Praise for the Maggie Brooklyn Mysteries

Vanishing Acts

"With likable characters and a fast-moving plot, this sequel to *Girl's Best Friend* is sure to be a hit. Perfect for fans . . . of Judy Moody or Allie Finkle and mystery fans who enjoy Sammy Keyes." —*SLJ*

"Witty and resourceful, compassionate and lovable, Maggie is just the kind of girl that you want your daughter to relate to. And she lives right next door." —*Park Slope Reader*

Girl's Best Friend

"A barking good mystery." —*Discovery Girls*

"Margolis leaves you wanting to look twice at every familiar gesture and setting." —Blue Balliett, author of *Chasing Vermeer*

"Maggie Brooklyn is a smart, funny, capable detective, and a *real kid*." —Adam Rex, author of *The True Meaning of Smekday*

"Leslie Margolis has found the perfect mix—a city story, a tween story, *and* a mystery that truly keeps you guessing." —Gordon Korman, author of *The 39 Clues: The Emperor's Code* and *Framed*

"The kind of good, solid mystery that slides neatly into a weekend or summer evening." —*BCCB*

"Maggie is a friendly and thoughtful narrator with a sharply logical mind; readers . . . will appreciate her intellect and bravery, and applaud her success." —*Publishers Weekly*

Books by Leslie Margolis

a maggie brooklyn mystery

Vanishing Acts

Leslie Margolis

BLOOMSBURY
NEW YORK   LONDON   NEW DELHI   SYDNEY

First published in the United States of America in January 2012
by Bloomsbury Children's Books
Paperback edition published in January 2013
www.bloomsbury.com

For information about permission to reproduce selections from this book, write to
Permissions, Bloomsbury Children's Books, 175 Fifth Avenue, New York, New York 10010

The Library of Congress has cataloged the hardcover edition as follows:
Margolis, Leslie.
Vanishing acts: a Maggie Brooklyn mystery / by Leslie Margolis. —1st U.S. ed.
p.   cm.
Summary: Life is confusing for seventh-grader Maggie, who must track down
a missing person and find out who is behind a string of dog eggings at the local
dog run, while also dealing with issues involving her brother and two of her friends.
ISBN 978-1-59990-536-5 (hardcover)
[1. Brothers and sisters—Fiction. 2. Twins—Fiction. 3. Junior high schools—Fiction. 4. Schools—Fiction.
5. Dogs—Fiction. 6. Missing persons—Fiction. 7. Mystery and detective stories.] I. Title.
PZ7.M33568Van 2012   [Fic]—dc23   2011018592

ISBN 978-1-59990-981-3 (paperback)

Book design by Nicole Gastonguay
Typeset by Westchester Book Composition
Printed in the U.S.A. by Thomson-Shore, Dexter, Michigan
2 4 6 8 10 9 7 5 3 1

All papers used by Bloomsbury Publishing, Inc., are natural, recyclable products
made from wood grown in well-managed forests. The manufacturing processes
conform to the environmental regulations of the country of origin.

Manufactured by Thomson-Shore, Dexter, MI (USA); RMA586LS775, November, 2012

For Lucy and Leo

Life imitates art far more often
than art imitates life.
—Oscar Wilde

Vanishing Acts

Chapter 1

. . .

Everything started in October on what I thought would be a typical Tuesday morning. It was cold. Not teeth-chattering, I-can't-feel-my-toes-and-my-nose-is-an-icicle cold, more like I-wish-I'd-already-broken-out-my-winter-coat-because-this-flimsy-fleece-isn't-doing-the-trick cold. Not even paired with my thick wool scarf—striped and hand-knit by my best friend, Lucy Phan.

Cool wind whistled through bare trees. Dried leaves danced at our feet as my twin brother, Finn, and I raced to school—running fast and running late because he'd pressed the snooze button on our alarm clock one too many times. (It was the third time that month, and I was *totally* counting!)

We were still a block from school when suddenly, out of nowhere, I got clobbered by a bloated guy in a top hat. He plowed right into me, making me scream, more from shock than any actual pain.

"What the . . ." I didn't finish my sentence because I don't like to swear. Not out loud, anyway.

As I blinked, he bounced to the ground, then rolled past a parked car, and, wait a second . . . People don't bounce—at least not more than once or twice. But this guy ricocheted across the sidewalk like a beach ball.

Then things got weird. Finn chased after the dude and picked him up with one hand and no obvious sign of struggle.

Once I got closer I realized why. He wasn't a bloated guy in a top hat at all. He was a life-size blow-up doll. Balloon-like and puffy, with eerily realistic-looking features: black mustache, rosy cheeks, thin lips, and tiny, pale pink ears. Someone had dressed him in a black suit with a matching tie. He looked like a chubby Charlie Chaplin, minus the derby cap and cane.

"You okay?" asked Finn.

"Fine." I brushed myself off. "Just surprised. And kinda creeped out."

"Just kinda?" Finn teased.

The two of us gazed at the doll, both thinking the same thing. Not because we're twins and we have super telepathic powers—we don't. Only because there's merely one possible reaction to this situation: extreme confusion.

"Where did he come from, do you think?"

"Don't know." Finn shook his head. "Nor do I know where he's going."

"Probably with those two." I pointed to two more blow-up dolls that tumbled by. These ones were made up to look like women, with long hair and long skirts trailing behind them as they drifted into oncoming traffic.

Someone in a Smart Car slammed on the brakes. Tires skidded to a loud angry stop and horns blared. Passersby on the sidewalk stopped passing by to stare as the pair continued down the street. They bounced buoyantly, totally oblivious to the hazards they caused.

Finn turned back to the doll in his hand. "Uh, think we should keep him?"

"It's not like we can bring him to school," I replied.

"Right. Good point." Finn let go.

The doll began to drift, but before it got very far I grabbed it and was surprised at how light it really was. "We can't just let him sail away. He could cause an accident. His friends almost did."

"So what do we do?" asked Finn. "We're totally gonna be late, and Ms. Murphy would never believe us if we told her why."

I looked around, noticed the empty trash can on the corner, and stuffed him in. "There!" I said.

The doll filled up the entire barrel. He peered straight at me with dull brown eyes. For someone with plastic features, he seemed surprisingly unhappy about his fate. The corners of his mouth turned down. His mustache drooped with disappointment. But what could I do?

"Sorry, dude, but it could've been worse. We could've deflated you," I said, before turning to Finn and calling, "Hurry up or we'll get detention!"

We ran the rest of the way. Missed the late bell, but managed to sneak into homeroom without anyone noticing.

"Plenty of time," Finn whispered as we slid into our seats.

"We got lucky," I replied as I retied my ponytail. "And tonight the alarm clock is moving to my side of the room."

Yes, Finn and I share a room but it's not as weird as it sounds. A giant bookcase divides his side from mine, and it offers plenty of privacy. Case in point—I didn't even notice him pressing the snooze button.

Finn shrugged. "Suit yourself."

After homeroom, I breezed through math, English, and social studies, almost like the wind propelled my schedule, too. So before I knew it, it was time for lunch.

Lucy was already waiting for me at my locker. She wore her long dark hair in a single braid, which told me she had music after school. (Her teacher is way strict and makes her wear her hair back so it doesn't get in the way.) And if I couldn't tell by her hair, she was also carrying her violin, because it doesn't fit in her locker.

"Hey, what's up?" she asked.

"Did you happen to run into any giant plastic dolls on the way to school this morning? Or, more to the point, did any giant plastic dolls happen to run into you?"

Lucy frowned and raised her hand to my forehead. "You feeling okay, Maggie?"

"I'm fine," I said. "Just—never mind." It seemed too complicated to explain—at least at the moment, while I was starving. "Let's eat. Are you carrying or buying?"

"Like you have to ask," she replied, holding up her lunch sack. "I'm packing spaghetti, but I'll come with you."

"Cool."

We headed outside with a swarm of other Fiske Street Junior High School seventh and eighth graders. Sixth graders aren't allowed to leave campus for lunch. And being a fairly new seventh grader, I still enjoyed the novelty of leaving school in the middle of the day.

We headed to Henry's so I could pick up a banh mi, which is a delicious Vietnamese sandwich that Lucy finds disgusting, even though she's half Vietnamese.

"I'll wait outside," she said once we got there. "I don't even like the smell."

"Someday you're going to want to eat more than spaghetti," I said.

"Ugh, you sound just like my mother!" said Lucy. "Last night she tried to get me to eat rice with clams in it, claiming it's my great-grandmother's long-lost recipe and that a single, mystically infused bowl will cause good luck. Can you think of a more obvious ploy?"

"You have no idea how good you have it!" I said. "My parents are working so much these days, they never cook. Finn and I have had pizza three nights in a row."

"That sounds so much better than having to eat leftovers from my parents' restaurant," said Lucy. "And I don't even like pizza."

After I got my sandwich, we headed back to the cafeteria and sat down at our usual table. But before I had the chance to nibble on even one sliver of pickled carrot, an eighth grader came up to me and asked, "Are you Maggie Brooklyn?"

She wasn't just any eighth grader, either. Her name was Charlotte Ginsburg, and she's totally popular. Not mean-girl, tease-you-to-your-face-or-trash-talk-you-behind-your-back popular—I don't think. She's just your standard, eighth grade, run-of-the-mill, pretty, cheerful kind of girl.

I looked up but didn't speak. I just didn't know what to say. Last time I saw Charlotte, she was walking down

Sixth Avenue with her three best friends—girly girls with bright smiles and shiny hair—their arms linked, taking up the whole sidewalk. They were so focused on one another that they didn't even notice me approach. No one moved over to make room, and I had to jump into the gutter to avoid running into them. And they weren't even being mean—just oblivious, because they could be. They're so used to people getting out of their way.

So obviously I couldn't figure out why she'd ventured to my table. For one thing, I'm in the seventh grade. Also, there's way less hair flipping, giggling, and gossiping on my side of the cafeteria.

Maybe she tripped and fell and hit her head this morning and now had amnesia. It was the only logical explanation, considering we were over a month into the new school year. Space at the cafeteria had been mapped out, invisible but powerful lines drawn. If you wanted to switch tables at this point, forget it. It was too late. Your friends were your friends, and there was nothing you could do about it for the rest of the semester—probably the rest of the year.

But it's not like I needed to explain this to Charlotte, who stood over me, puzzled and waiting for a response.

A response other than a confused, silent gaze, I mean.

"Yes, I'm Maggie Brooklyn," I said finally.

"The dog-walking detective?" she asked, her tone all business.

Suddenly everything became clear. I recently found some missing dogs. And not just some—Finn says I need to quit being so modest. I rescued seven dogs from an evil dognapper posing as an identical-twin veterinarian, and lots of people found out about it, which made me legitimately popular for an entire week, then just semipopular the week after that.

Three weeks later everything went back to normal, meaning most people didn't really notice me. Which is not just okay by me—I actually prefer it. I love solving mysteries, and being inconspicuous helps in a major way.

I'm tall, but not too tall, with long, dark, wavy hair and eyes that are green or hazel, depending on who you ask. Basically, I'm your average twelve-year-old girl, and no one expects that an average twelve-year-old girl could be capable of serious detective work.

"I'm not a professional or anything," I told Charlotte. "I don't even have business cards. But I do walk a few dogs after school, and I have solved some mysteries." (By "some" I meant two, because besides finding the missing dogs, I'd also tracked down my landlady's long-lost fortune.)

"That's good, because I need some help, and my dog does, too," said Charlotte.

"I'm not allowed to walk any more dogs," I said. "I already have four clients, and that barely gives me enough time for homework."

"I don't need you to walk Mister Fru Fru," said Charlotte. "I do that. I just need you to figure out who egged him this morning!"

"Wait, your dog got egged?" I asked.

"Your dog's name is 'Mister Fru Fru'?" Lucy marveled.

I kicked her under the table.

"What?" she asked with a shrug. "It's a legitimate question."

As Charlotte glared, her pink lips formed into one thin glossy line of impatience. "Yeah, I named my dog Mister Fru Fru. You want to make something of it?"

"Nope." Lucy looked down at her spaghetti and twirled another forkful.

"Tell me what happened," I said. "Like, step by step." I pulled out my brand-new dog-walking/crime-fighting notepad. It reads "Doggie Deets" across the top, so it's multipurpose.

Charlotte huffed out a small breath. "We were walking into the park before school, as usual, when this small white blur whizzed past me, and the next thing I knew, Mister Fru Fru was whimpering and covered in egg."

"That's horrible," I said.

"No kidding," she replied. "And guess what else—Mister Fru Fru isn't the only victim. I asked around, and it turns out that *lots* of dogs got egged in the park last weekend. It's, like, an epidemic or something." She pulled her hair up into a loose bun and then changed her mind and dropped it down again. "So, can you figure out who's behind it?"

"I can try," I said. "Where in the park were you, exactly?"

"I entered at Ninth Street, near where I live."

"And what time were you there?"

"Seven thirty, I think. No, I had to wait for my manicure to dry before I left the house, so it was probably closer to seven forty-five." Charlotte looked down at her lavender-with-a-hint-of-sparkle nails. "Although a couple got smudged, so I must have left too early. Maybe at seven forty?"

I appreciated how seriously she was taking this.

"Do you know any of the other victims?" I asked. "Because I'd like to speak to them."

"To the dogs?" asked Charlotte. She tilted her head and looked at me with wide green eyes. "You can do that?"

I stared at her hard, trying to figure out if she was making fun of me. Amazingly, she didn't seem to be.

"I mean the owners," I replied, as delicately as possible.

"Oh, yeah, of course. No, I don't. But go to the park and ask around. Everybody's talking about it."

Charlotte walked away without thanking me. Not that I'd done anything yet, except take notes. I stared down at them, trying to figure out where to begin.

Doggie Deets

Mister Fru Fru egged at 7:40 a.m. on Tuesday, Ninth Street entrance to Prospect Park.

Before I could make sense of anything, Sonya ran over and sat across from me with an excited thump. "We've got news."

"Big news," Beatrix added, sliding in right next to her.

"They're filming a Seth Ryan movie here!" yelled Sonya, tapping her hands on the table, drumroll style. "And we're going to be in it!"

Chapter 2

• • •

If I were the type to travel in a pack, like a wolf or one of those girls with a bunch of best friends, Sonya and Beatrix would be in it, no question. They're in the seventh grade, too, and just as sweet and funny as Lucy. But since I am a one-best-friend type of girl, they're the next best thing.

And that's okay, because I don't think they'd want to be best, best friends with me, either, since I'm not obsessed with Seth Ryan.

Like most kids I know, he's my favorite movie star, for the obvious reasons: cute, a great actor, and he donated the proceeds of his last movie to the ASPCA. In other words, he's a puppy lover with puppy-dog eyes.

I've seen most of his movies. The last two I even went to on opening night.

But it's not like I'd start a Seth Ryan fan club.

Or launch a website devoted to his life and work.

Or design T-shirts with his face on them.

Or have meetings after school twice a week to plan even more Seth Ryan superfan–related activities.

Yet that's exactly what Beatrix and Sonya have been doing.

Beatrix has been into Seth Ryan for over a year. For Sonya, he's a new obsession. She'd only just recently replaced the unicorn posters on her bedroom walls with pinups of him.

"Who's Seth Ryan?" I asked with a straight face.

"Not funny, Maggie," said Beatrix. "You can't joke about the most famous movie star in the world. He's off-limits!"

"How are you guys going to be in his movie?" asked Lucy.

"Not just Sonya and me," said Beatrix. "All of us. They're filming in the neighborhood and they need extras, immediately."

"That sounds amazing," Lucy said.

"Almost too amazing," I added.

"That's exactly what I thought," said Sonya. "But I know it's true, because it's all over the Internet."

"Isn't that where you read they were tearing down our school to put in a giant cupcake factory?" I asked.

"It wasn't a giant cupcake factory," Sonya replied. "It was a regular-size factory that specialized in baking giant cupcakes."

"Obviously," said Lucy, smiling at me.

"You guys, this is totally legit," said Sonya as she unpacked her lunch. "I promise. I walked by Second Street on my way to school, and it's already closed to regular traffic. This giant truck rolled up and unloaded six humongous trailers. You know—the kind movie stars use as dressing rooms. And then another truck came, and it was filled with giant lights and movie cameras."

This wasn't hugely shocking. People film stuff in our neighborhood all the time. Especially on Second Street. In the past six months, they'd roped off the street for a Tom Cruise movie and a Trident gum commercial. But as for the rest of it? It seemed too good to be true.

"If they really needed extras, don't you think they would've figured it out before today?" I asked.

"They had," said Beatrix. "Or at least they thought they had. They were going to use a crowd in a box."

"What's that?" asked Lucy.

"It's an inflatable crowd," Beatrix explained. "It's when they use blow-up people to save money so they don't have to deal with real extras."

"Inflatable extras are much less complicated," said Sonya. "Except on days with high winds."

"They all blew away," Beatrix said. "And there's no time to get new plastic."

Suddenly everything clicked into place. "So that

explains that puffy dude that plowed into me this morning."

"Huh?" asked my friends.

I told them about my run-in with the blow-up doll. "We saw a few, but I had no idea they were part of a whole gang."

"There were thirty, apparently," said Beatrix. "Kind of an expensive mistake."

"So where's the doll?" asked Lucy.

"We stuffed him in a trash can on Garfield," I explained. "Finn wanted to keep him, but I said no way."

"Finn is so funny," said Lucy.

My brother is a lot of things: quiet, smart, and good at soccer and video games and making omelets. Sweet when he wants to be, and, at times, slightly clueless. But funny? I don't think so.

"Think the dummy's still there?" asked Sonya. "He'd be a cool addition to our collection of Seth Ryan memorabilia."

"I don't think a blow-up doll would fit in the scrapbook," said Beatrix.

"I mean if we deflated him," Sonya said. "Obviously."

"He was huge," I said. "Taller than me and probably as wide as Finn and me put together, so even flat and folded it would be a stretch."

"We need to get a third scrapbook anyway," Sonya said.

"Unless we just move all of the existing stuff to a bigger binder," said Beatrix. She turned to Lucy and me. "We can't seem to agree."

Lucy and I grinned at each other, not at all surprised. It seemed like Beatrix and Sonya disagreed about everything relating to Seth Ryan: which movie was his best, how often they should e-mail him, where to hold their next fan club meeting, whether or not they should continue calling themselves a fan club, considering the fact that they were the only two members . . .

"And it's not like we can vote on it," said Sonya. "We need a third person to break the tie, but there's no way we're going to try asking anyone at school again."

Last month, Beatrix and Sonya tried recruiting new kids to their club. Lucy and I were obvious choices, but we're both too busy. So they put up a bunch of signs around campus. It seemed like a no-brainer, since every girl here, practically, is in love with Seth Ryan. Boys like him, too. They'd never say so out loud, but their hairstyles prove it.

Of course, it didn't work out so well. Within an hour, their signs got covered with mean graffiti. People drew funny mustaches and devil's horns on his close-ups. They blacked out his eyes and half his teeth and scrawled obnoxious messages like *Seth Ryan Super Nerds* and *Dorks R Us!* and *This is Dum*, which is particularly insulting, because obviously there is nothing dumber than being called dumb by someone who can't even spell the word "dumb."

The takeaway being, it's cool to like Seth Ryan—almost everyone at school does—but it's not cool to be in an official fan club. All admiring must be done in an unofficial capacity. Beatrix and Sonya learned that the hard way.

"I'll bet they need guys, too," said Lucy. "Maybe Finn wants to sign up."

"They didn't specify, but I'm sure they do. You should definitely ask him," said Beatrix.

I shook my head. "There's no way. If I even mention the possibility, he'll laugh in my face. Last month after I rented *Vampire's Retreat* he made fun of me for a week."

"Maybe I'll ask him," said Lucy. "I don't think he'd laugh at me."

And before I could stop her, she'd jumped up from the table and was gone, her single braid bouncing on her back as she hurried across the cafeteria.

I turned to my friends. "Have you guys noticed Lucy acting weird lately?"

"Yes," said Sonya. "But no weirder than usual. So are you in?"

"It sounds fun, but I have to work after school."

"This is work," said Beatrix. "I heard they're paying eighty bucks a day just to stand around and be on camera. Filming starts tomorrow. The movie is called *Vanished*. Since we're under eighteen, we've got to get our parents' permission, but I already printed out extra release forms." She slammed a piece of paper down in front of me. "Here. Have your parents read and sign it. And report to work tomorrow at four p.m. sharp. Don't be late. Who knows how many people are going to show? Hundreds, I'm sure."

I looked down at the form. It had lots of fine print. I looked back up at my friends. "I don't think I can do it. I'm pretty busy with my dogs, and I didn't even tell you about my new mystery."

Sonya stared at me, her big brown eyes even wider than usual. "That's really cool, but can't it wait a few days? How many times do you think an opportunity like this is going to come up?"

Beatrix nodded. "Please sign up. It's going to be crazy fun!"

I told them I'd think about it, figuring Beatrix knew what she was talking about. Being an extra did seem like it would be crazy fun.

At least that's what I'd thought at the time.

Turns out we were only half right.

Chapter 3

. . .

There are many different ways to remove gum from the fur of a dog. Peanut butter or ice, for example, and a purple, stinky solution called "Gum-B-Gone." Unfortunately none of them worked on Nofarm, the scrappy fifty-pound mutt I was trying to clean after school that day, so I had to resort to scissors.

Nofarm sat calmly for me as I snipped the strawberry-flavored, bubble-fun-encrusted fur off his back. Then I ran my fingers through his coat, doing my best to cover up the small pink bald spot. By the time I finished, you couldn't see the skin.

"Good thing you're so furry," I said, giving him a quick pat before clipping on his leash. This was the third piece of gum I'd had to cut off him this month. And I don't even know whom to blame. Beckett, the mischievous toddler he lives with, or Beckett's moms, who clearly let him get away with too much.

Luckily, Nofarm doesn't seem to blame anyone. Or care. Or maybe he doesn't even notice.

We took a twenty-minute walk, he did his thing, and I brought him home. Easy-peasy. Or it would've been, if I were the type of girl to characterize things as easy-peasy, but I am not.

"One dog down, three to go. See you tomorrow, Nofarm," I said, giving his neck a good scratch before closing and locking the door behind me.

Next I headed to Bean's place. I try not to play favorites among my clients—it seems wrong, unprofessional, somehow. But if I did, Bean would most definitely not be one.

When I got to his place, I found his owner, Cassie, kneeling in the living room, brushing Bean's fur. Bean looked lovely—her hair silky, smooth, and shiny white, as usual. Meanwhile, Cassie seemed frantic. More so than usual, I mean; maybe because her red hair sat atop her head like a particularly thorny tumbleweed.

"Hi!" I said. "No work today?"

"I had to stay home," said Cassie. "Emergency."

"Is everything okay?" I asked.

"Not really," said Cassie. "But I'm glad you're here. Do you notice anything different about Bean?" She stared at me closely with wide blue eyes. "Does she seem . . . strange?"

I stared at Cassie's dog—a six-pound, fluffy Maltese. Her sparkly pink nails matched the ribbons in her hair. Her cardigan was pink and green striped—custom-made to order and hand-knit, courtesy of Lucy, who'd just launched her new line of pet sweaters on Etsy. (She was making a killing on Bean's wardrobe alone.)

"She looks perfectly normal to me," I said.

Cassie exhaled. "That is a huge relief. You'll never guess what happened this morning—Bean almost got egged!"

"At the park?" I asked. "Were you near the Ninth Street entrance?"

"You heard about it?" asked Cassie. "When I called the police and demanded that they warn everyone in Brooklyn, it sounded like they weren't taking me seriously. I guess they must've been laughing about something else."

"I didn't hear about Bean's egging," I said. "But the same thing happened to my friend Charlotte's dog. Well, she's not my friend, exactly. Just someone I go to school with who wants my help. She's an eighth grader, and kind of—"

"It was the scariest thing I've ever experienced in my entire short life," said Cassie. "I'm talking major trauma. This is worse than when our shipment of Jimmy Choos came in the wrong color."

"Your what?" I asked.

"They're shoes," said Cassie. "We needed them for a big photo shoot. You know I'm a stylist, right?"

"I didn't, actually."

"Anyway, that mistake cost three people their jobs. No big deal. But this? It's a much graver situation. I'm just so worried about poor Bean. She's got to be so traumatized, because you know how she is about keeping her fur perfectly clean and white. She cries whenever she steps in mud."

"Really?" I asked.

"Well, I cry whenever she steps in mud," Cassie said with a cough. "But only because I know that Bean is suffering in silence. Anyway, now I'm worried she's got PTSD."

"And that is . . . what?"

"PTSD stands for post-traumatic stress disorder. It happens when people experience great trauma. Terrorist attacks, war, kidnappings—"

I shook my head. Even for Cassie, this seemed nuts. "Can dogs get PTSD?" I asked.

"Of course they can! Although I suppose you might call it PPTSD. *Pet* post-traumatic stress disorder."

I considered Bean, currently sniffing a dust bunny in the corner. "You did say she *almost* got egged, correct?"

"They only missed her by an inch." Cassie held up

her thumb and forefinger, in case I'd never seen a ruler before.

"They?" I asked.

"They, he, she, whoever." Cassie shrugged. "I don't really know who did it."

"Think, though," I said. "Are there any details you can remember? I need to find whoever's responsible, and so far I don't have much to go on."

Cassie handed Bean over to me, then sat cross-legged on the floor and closed her eyes. She sealed her lips together and breathed in and out through her nose. I supposed this was her concentration pose; I hoped she'd start talking soon, because it was getting late.

"I remember laughter," she said, finally.

"Laughter?"

"Yes, laughter," she repeated.

I pulled my notebook from my backpack and wrote this down. "Whose laughter?"

"No idea."

"Do you know where it was coming from? Any clue? Any small detail could help."

"I don't know about the egg, but as for the laughter— I think it came from above," said Cassie. "At least it sounded that way."

I added "From above" with a question mark to my notes.

"Please give me your honest, professional opinion about Bean," Cassie said. "Do you think she'll ever recover?"

I raised Bean to my face so I could look her in the eye. Bean stared right back at me, letting out a low growl. I put her down gently. "I think she'll be back to herself in no time," I replied as I took her yellow polka-dotted leash out of the closet.

"The problem is, the symptoms can lay dormant for years," said Cassie. "Don't worry, though. I'm doing what I can. I stayed home from work so I could bathe her. I've also called a pet therapist, who's coming at five thirty to begin counseling Bean through the trauma. And I've signed her up for Doga as well. I hear it's a great stress reliever."

"Doga?" I asked.

"Dog-yoga," Cassie replied, like it was obvious. Then she held up a tiny headband and a matching pair of Bean-size yoga pants. "Look what I got her. Cute, right? Our first class is tomorrow morning. It's supposed to do wonders for her flexibility, too."

I knew better than to question it. "Um, should I still take her out, or do you think she's too . . . fragile right now?"

"No, please, take her for a walk!" said Cassie. "I don't want her regular routine interrupted. That's why

I decided to put her in bows, because it's Tuesday, and she always wears her fur up on Tuesdays."

"Good thinking." I struggled to keep a straight face. Dog eggings were serious, and seriously horrifying. But weekly hairstyles? Well, they were horrifying in a different sense.

"Please keep her away from Ninth Street. And could you put her in this, too?" Cassie handed me a yellow rain slicker. "You do have an umbrella, right?"

I glanced out the window. The wind had blown away all the clouds, leaving blue sky and a golden late-afternoon sunshine. "No, but I don't think it's going to rain."

"The umbrella is to shield her from another attack," said Cassie. "Because what if this wasn't some random act of violence? What if someone's after poor Bean?"

"I really don't think—"

"You can take mine. It's the pink one with puppies on it—by the front door."

I grabbed the first umbrella I saw.

"No, the one on the left."

I glanced at the umbrella in my hand. "This one has puppies on it," I said.

"But it's magenta," Cassie said. "I'm talking *true* pink."

Chapter 4

. . .

On our short walk, Bean acted uptight.

High-strung.

Nervous.

Hostile to other dogs.

And people.

Even birds.

Also? She snapped at a butterfly.

In short, Bean acted like herself. But we made it back without any major incidents. Something I reported to Cassie, who'd been anxiously waiting for me by the front door.

"That's a huge relief. Thank you, Maggie!" She gave me a squishy hug that left traces of fruity perfume on my fleece.

My next client lived right upstairs. Dog-Milo is a cute, sweet, mellow puggle.

Ironically, we ran right into boy-Milo as soon as we got outside.

My friend Milo is also cute, sweet, and mellow, just like his canine namesake. He's also tall and thin and quiet, with perfectly floppy brown hair. I used to admire Milo from afar, and now I admire him from a-near, because we hang out all the time.

I guess one could still say I have a secret crush on him. Except now Finn and Lucy and Sonya and Beatrix know about my feelings, so it's not exactly a secret. Also, Milo kind of knows, too. I think. But that's okay, because I have this sneaking suspicion that he's got a not-so-secret crush on me as well.

At least he acts that way. He smiles at me whenever I see him. And he's often hanging around, waiting for me to invite him places. Like right now. I know for a fact that Milo meets his chess tutor after school on Tuesdays, all the way on the other side of the neighborhood. Yet here he was, right in front of the building where two of my clients live. Just like he is almost every afternoon.

Not in a stalker way. More like an I'm-your-boyfriend-and-we-had-plans-to-meet-up way. Even though we never officially talked about it (the meeting up or the boyfriend thing).

"Hey," he said, pretending to be surprised. "What are you doing here?"

"Working." I pointed to the puggle as if Milo hadn't met him ten times before. "You remember Milo the dog, right?"

"This is where he lives?" asked Milo, falling in step with me. "I keep forgetting."

Milo is a good guy, but a bad liar. Not that I'd call him on it. "What are you up to?" I asked instead.

Milo shrugged. "Not much. Hanging out. I had chess today. And then my grandma needed something from the pharmacy around the corner. She doesn't like the one by our apartment, so I always have to walk up here. But her prescription wasn't ready, so I was just—"

I bit my bottom lip to keep from smiling too wide. Milo's so cute when he goes on and on about why he happened to be standing here—like, he makes so many elaborate and complicated excuses, it's obvious they're fake. Unless his grandma needs a new prescription every single day, which I suppose is possible, but highly unlikely. Today I cut him off before he got *too* carried away.

"Want to come to the park with me? Charlotte Ginsburg's dog got egged this morning and I'm on the case."

"Her dog got egged?" asked Milo.

"Yup," I said. "And it's worse than that. Mister Fru Fru isn't the only victim."

"Charlotte's dog's name is 'Mister Fru Fru'?" asked Milo.

"I know," I replied. "Bean just narrowly escaped an egg attack this morning."

"Who'd egg such a tiny, defenseless little dog?" Milo asked. Then, after thinking about it for a minute, he added, "Do you think it could be someone she's tried to attack?"

"Don't know," I replied. "But I don't think so. Yes, Bean's got some personality issues, but Mister Fru Fru is a sweetheart."

"You know him?" asked Milo.

"Nope. But that's what Charlotte's friends tell me."

Milo smiled at me. "You did a background check on a dog?"

I pulled my notebook from my backpack and flipped to the page on Mister Fru Fru. "Not just any dog," I replied. "A forty-seven-pound black Standard Poodle sporting a royal blue collar and a matching leash."

"Impressive," said Milo.

"I believe in being thorough." I put my notebook away and readjusted my backpack. "Anyway, apparently there've been a bunch of egg attacks this weekend."

"Like, how many?"

"I'm not sure. That's why we need to investigate."

Yes, I said "we," as in Milo and me. Like we were a couple, even though we are not. Yet. And I'm not saying it will definitely happen. But it could. I think. In fact, if things continued the way they were going, it probably would.

I think and hope so, anyway.

We walked in silence for a while, but not an awkward, agonizing silence. It was more like a we-are-so-used-to-this-and-cool-with-each-other-so-we-don't-have-to-speak-all-the-time silence.

Once we got closer to Ninth Street, I kicked into detective mode. "We need to talk to as many dog owners as possible," I told him. "So let's split up."

"Can I borrow some paper?" he asked.

"What for?"

"So I can take notes."

"Oh, sure." We stopped at the park entrance so I could tear off three pages from my notebook. I handed them over with my spare pen.

When Milo reached for it, our fingers touched. I didn't let go of my end of the pen immediately, and we smiled at each other, and then both looked away, embarrassed. And silent, because what do you say after such a perfect moment? There are no words.

"I'll take the boxer peeing on that stroller," Milo said, pointing toward the playground.

"Okay, cool. See you in a bit."

I headed in the opposite direction, pausing so dog-Milo could relieve himself in the grass. Once he finished, I walked up to Jane, a full-time dog walker. She walks about eighteen dogs over the course of a day, but at the moment, she had only three.

"Hey, Maggie," she said. "And hi, little Milo." She bent down to pet Milo, and I pet her three dogs—Clover, Scout, and Eminem.

Jane used to be pretty hostile toward me—afraid I'd take away all her business, even though I'd always assured her I'm a small operation. But she warmed up to me after she heard about last month's rescue mission.

"Hey, have you heard anything about this week-end's egg attacks?" I asked.

"Heard about them?" asked Jane. "Clover was a victim on Sunday morning. She'd just treed a squirrel when she got egged in the face."

"Any idea who threw it?"

"Nope," said Jane. "It's like it came from nowhere."

"Did you happen to hear any noise?" I asked.

"You mean besides the slap of the egg and poor Clover's yelp?"

Just hearing that brought tears to my eyes. What kind of jerk would attack an innocent dog? I sniffed and blinked hard, knowing I needed to remain calm. Detectives have got to keep their cool, act rationally, and think clearly, without letting their emotions get in the way. That's what I read somewhere, anyway.

"I only ask because the same thing happened to Cassie's dog, and she heard laughter."

Jane shook her head. "There was no laughter."

"Interesting," I replied, taking down some notes. "And what is Clover? A chocolate Lab?"

"Yes," said Jane. "That's exactly what she is."

I wrote that down, too. Out of the corner of my eye I spied a woman walking her two beagles. I said good-bye to Jane and ran to catch up with her.

Turns out the woman's dogs hadn't been hit. And she had no idea what I was talking about. But the guy standing next to her overheard me and wanted to talk. His name was Milton. He had a purple mohawk and a black and white springer spaniel named David, and he was still fuming over his dog's egg attack from this morning.

"It happened at eight a.m. The craziest thing. And I swear I saw a guy in a black T-shirt appear from nowhere and then run for the woods."

"What do you mean he appeared from nowhere?" I asked.

"Just that—it's like he was magical."

"But that's impossible," I said.

"That's what I thought, too," said Milton. He wiggled his fingers in front of his eyes. "Totally trippy."

"Well, what did he look like?" I asked.

"Like someone I wanted to pummel for egging my dog!" Milton replied, not very helpfully.

It was already five o'clock by the time we finished talking—dangerously close to my weeknight curfew. And I still had one more dog to walk. I found boy-Milo and told him I had to go. "Did you find any other victims?" I asked.

"Yup," he said. "You?"

"Yeah—a couple."

Milo handed me a piece of paper.

"What's this?" I asked.

"An incident report," he said. "I'm not quite done, but here's what I have so far."

"Thanks," I said.

"You're welcome. It's no biggie," he replied with a shrug.

Then he turned around and jogged off without even saying good-bye. Which is strange, because usually he walks me home.

I looked down at the page. Milo's writing started out neat and boxy; then halfway through his report it morphed into sloppy cursive, like he had to struggle to keep up with the interviewees.

I squinted at the note, really wanting to make sure I made out those final words properly. Because it looked like Milo had not merely collected evidence—he'd also asked me on a date.

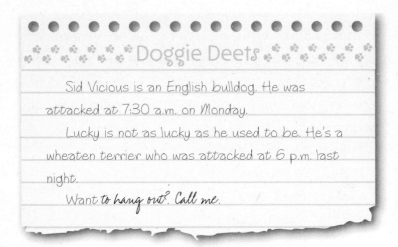

Doggie Deets

Sid Vicious is an English bulldog. He was attacked at 7:30 a.m. on Monday.

Lucky is not as lucky as he used to be. He's a wheaten terrier who was attacked at 6 p.m. last night.

Want to hang out? Call me.

Chapter 5

◆ ◆ ◆

Dog-Milo and I ran home as fast as his little puggle legs would carry him. After checking his water bowl and locking up at Parminder's place, I took my landlady's dog, Preston, for a quick spin around the block. Then I headed straight upstairs to my apartment.

At my desk in my room I studied my notes, looking for patterns or connections or clues, or, ideally, all three.

Except my eyes kept narrowing in on the bottom of Milo's note, making it hard to focus on the eggings. I wondered if maybe this would finally happen. Milo and me, I mean. I pictured us strolling through the park, holding hands. Slipping notes into each other's lockers. Sharing one bucket of popcorn at the movies. Sledding in the park after the first snowstorm, and later that night sipping hot cocoa by the fire. (Not that either of us has a fireplace. But let's not get too caught up on the details.)

How perfect and romantic and spontaneous to finally ask me out on one of my doggie deets!

At least that's what I thought before the doubt crept in.

Maybe when Milo said, "Want to hang out?" he meant it in a completely non-romantic, strictly "we're just friends" kind of way.

Hanging out doesn't have to be a date. I hang out with my friends all the time.

I put Milo's note aside, because I didn't want to spend all night analyzing its true meaning. Not when I had a mystery to solve. I needed to focus on the egg attacks. And since my notes weren't getting me very far, I needed a new place to look.

One thing about Brooklyn is, a lot of writers live here. And where there are a lot of writers, there are lots and lots of blogs. I figured someone must be documenting the egg attacks. And a quick Google search told me a few people were.

I found a whole blog devoted to the attacks.

I read up on Paco, the Great Dane who was egged on Saturday afternoon at four o'clock. His owner, Jed, reported three eggs fired. The first one missed; the second Jed managed to deflect with his hand; the third they tried to dodge, but in the end, Paco got hit in the back. Like the attacks I already knew about, the eggs seemed to come from nowhere, with no warning.

Then there was Hemingway, a big white husky, egged at seven thirty on Thursday morning. "Just a single egg seemed to drop from the sky," the owner reported. "No one got hurt, but I got egg all over my new wingtips."

Pretty's spiked leather collar was now encrusted in egg, thanks to an attack on Friday at 7:14 a.m. His owner, Harry, spotted someone leaping out of a tree and running for the woods. He chased this person, but lost him or her.

I tried to make sense of my notes, to find some sort of pattern, either in the style of attack, the dog breed, or the time of day. Sure, Harry described his dog's attack in the same way Milton had, but other than that, there weren't many similarities.

However, all of the eggings took place on the weekend or early in the morning or late in the day—so I could at least conclude that the egger had a traditional nine-to-five type of job. Or maybe he or she or they were in school. Or maybe the egger had nothing to do all day and just waited until the park was most populated with dogs, since most dog owners do have jobs or go to school.

This person liked to climb trees. Or at least, he or she was good at it. Also, the egger ran fast.

Lots of people go to school or have jobs or don't and can run fast and climb trees, so I wasn't really narrowing my suspects down very far.

I drew a map of that section of the park: playground on the right, Long Meadow straight ahead, lots of trees and lots of brush. In other words, plenty of places to hide.

When I heard my mom's voice a few minutes later, I jumped.

I turned to find her standing in my doorway, still in her navy blue suit from work. She'd changed her shoes though, unless she'd started wearing bunny slippers to the office and I just hadn't noticed.

"How's your homework?" she asked.

"Great," I said. And I wasn't lying. Not really. My homework *was* great—and sitting untouched in my notebook. Pristine, with no fingerprints, wrinkles, or wrong answers. Only, there weren't any right answers, either. I hadn't begun.

Not that I was about to admit this to my mom. She's cool, but strict when it comes to schoolwork. One of those moms who wants to know what Finn and I learned each day. And she's way into scheduling our free time, too. I'm lucky she lets me walk dogs, and I'm only allowed to keep it up if I make it home by five thirty every night and keep my grades up.

"I didn't hear you come in," I said.

"You must be concentrating pretty hard, because you forgot to set the table."

"Is it already time for dinner?" I checked my watch.

"It's okay. I did it, and everyone else is already sitting down."

I closed my notebook and followed my mom into the dining room. Finn and our dad had already started in on the turkey meatloaf.

"Hi, Mags," said my dad. "Finn was just telling me about your strange morning."

"Huh?" I asked, since I hadn't told him about Charlotte and the new dog-egger case.

"I mean the blow-up dolls," said Finn.

"Oh, that. I almost forgot." Sometimes it amazes me how much can happen in a single day.

"Did you say blow-up doll?" asked our mom with a look of alarm.

I told her all about the inflatable crowd. "It was supposed to be a part of the new Seth Ryan movie. They're filming on Second Street starting tomorrow."

My father grinned. "I was wondering how long it would be before you found out about that."

"You mean you knew?" I asked.

"Sure. Jenna Beasely came around with a petition trying to get the location moved last month," he explained.

"Who?" I asked.

"You know Jenna," said my mom. "She's my friend from law school. We all had brunch at that great place on Vanderbilt last summer."

"There's no such thing as a great brunch place," said Finn. "Which is exactly what I tried to tell you last week at Rio Nadres."

"It got amazing reviews online," said Mom.

"Did they mention that you have to wait for over an hour before being served a lousy plate of runny eggs and cold potatoes?"

Making Finn wait around for food when he's hungry is pretty much the worst thing you can do to my brother, which is why he was still grumpy about the brunch— and brunch as a category in general—a week later.

I turned back to my dad. "Wait, did you say she was trying to move the location?"

"Yup. She wanted to get the entire production banned from Brooklyn."

I gasped. "Why would anyone do that?"

"If you lived on Second Street, you'd understand. They film things all the time there," Mom said. "And it's plenty inconvenient. Basically, they take over the entire block, roping off both sides so you can't even park on your own street. Besides the noise, you have to deal with the bright lights, and sometimes they shoot in the middle of the night, making sleep impossible. That's what Jenna says, anyway. We're lucky we've never had to find out for ourselves."

My mom was right—no one had filmed anything on Garfield that I could remember, but I wished they would. It seemed so cool.

"Who wouldn't want to be inconvenienced if it meant possibly running into Seth Ryan?" I asked.

"I think you have your answer in Jenna," said my dad. "But you don't need to worry about it, because she wasn't able to stop them."

"Good," I said. "Because they need extras, and I was hoping to sign up."

I pulled the release form out of my back pocket, unfolded it, and gave it to my dad.

I'd decided that my friends were right—this was a once-in-a-lifetime opportunity, and it was worth juggling homework and dog walking for. Somehow I'd make it work. If I was allowed to, that is. I figured I had a better shot of getting permission from my dad, since he works in film. Kind of. He doesn't do anything cool like make Seth Ryan movies—he just films documentaries: movies about stuff that's true, which are very different from reality television (according to him).

"Let me see that before you sign it," said my mom, holding out her hand.

"Oh, I'm not planning on signing anything yet," said my dad.

"You're not?" I asked.

Yes, this afternoon I wasn't sure if I had time to be an extra, but now that my parents might not let me— suddenly it was all I wanted to do.

"Not until we both take a good look at it." My dad took his reading glasses out of his pocket and slipped them on. "This looks pretty standard," he said after a few moments, handing it over to my mom. "I have no problem with it."

"Will you promise this won't interfere with your schoolwork?" asked my mom, predictably.

"It won't," I replied with a sigh.

"And what about your business?" she asked. "You did make a commitment. Lots of people depend on you."

"And animals do, too. I know that. There's time for both. Anyway, how can I pass this up? How many times in my life will I get the chance to meet Seth Ryan?"

My father laughed. "I know this is exciting, and hopefully it'll be fun, too, but I don't think you're actually going to meet Seth Ryan. These superstars exist in a different reality. He's not going to be hanging around the extras tent."

"I'll get to stay in a tent? How cool!"

"It's not actually a tent," my dad said. "Just an expression."

"Well, it's still cool," I said. "Want me to do the dishes?"

My mom stared at me. "You really want this, huh?" she asked.

"Maybe," I replied, standing up and grabbing her plate. "Or perhaps I'm just being *extra* helpful."

Back in my room that night, I studied Milo's note. I was 90 percent sure he actually wanted to hang out, and there was only one way to find out for sure. I picked up the phone and started dialing his number. I made it about halfway through before freezing.

Suddenly the image of Jasper Michaelson flashed into my mind. Jasper was a perfectly nice girl who moved to New Jersey last summer. She was pretty, too: straight blond hair, heavy bangs, green eyes, invisible braces. Before she moved, she called here looking for Finn, and not just once—three times in the same night. Finn was out for the first call, so I ended up speaking to her.

When he got home, I gave him the message, and he grunted something that might've been "thanks," but I wasn't listening that closely. Then he went into the kitchen and had some chips. When the phone rang a little later, I answered it. "Hey, Jasper," I'd said. And Finn began gesticulating wildly—eyes wide and arms waving.

"Are you choking?" I whispered to him.

"I'm not here," he whispered back.

"But you are," I said.

"Tell her I'm not!" he insisted.

"But she can probably hear you," I replied.

Finn covered his ears with his hands and walked out of the room, forcing me to lie, something I can't stand doing.

"He's still not back," I said. "But I'll have him call you when he is."

Once I hung up, Finn raced back into the room, asking, "Why did you do that?"

"What do you mean? I did exactly what you asked me to do."

"Not exactly. Why'd you tell her I'd call her back?"

"Because I'm a nice, normal person."

Finn just shook his head and walked away. I don't know why Jasper called that day, and neither does Finn, because he never called her back. Not even after she called the third time later that night and I had to lie for him all over again. Finn and I never talked about it, and I certainly didn't ask him. I didn't have to. I could tell by the way Jasper smiled at me the next day at school—sheepish and embarrassed. When I found out she moved away, my first thought was she probably left Brooklyn because she couldn't stand the humiliation.

I felt so bad for her at the time. But more powerful than that was the desire to never be like her.

That's why I didn't call Milo. He only just asked me. I could wait a day. Maybe two days. I didn't want to seem desperate. And anyway, what if I was totally wrong? Perhaps he didn't want me to call at all. We were investigating the dog-egging case together, so maybe I'd misunderstood. It's entirely possible that he'd been in the middle of taking notes about a dog named "Call me."

Chapter 6

. . .

Not only did my parents sign the release form for me later that night, they also signed a copy for Finn.

Yes, Finn, my brother.

The same brother who thinks Seth Ryan and all Seth Ryan fans are super dorky had volunteered to be an extra in the new Seth Ryan movie.

I asked him why, but "I have my reasons" is all he'd tell me; totally mysterious. I could not figure it out. Not until I found him waiting for me at Lucy's locker after school the next day.

"This is some elaborate plan to make fun of me and my friends, right?" I asked. "You're just hanging around so you can gather material. Make teasing us that much more authentic."

"What are you talking about?" asked Finn.

"Just admit it." I punched him in the arm for even thinking the thought.

"Ow!" said Finn, backing away from me. "Cut it out."

"I think he really wants to be an extra," said Lucy, sneaking up from behind. Her hair was freshly brushed, lips shiny with gloss. She'd changed into her favorite black pants and purple hoodie.

"Oh, you got dressed up for Seth Ryan?" I asked.

"Something like that," Lucy replied. "Let's go."

"What about Beatrix and Sonya?" asked Finn.

"Their plan was to sprint to Second Street as soon as the bell rang," Lucy explained. "So they're probably already there."

As we headed over, Finn asked Lucy, "How was your math test?"

"Good," she replied. "I think. Although last time I thought I did well on a test I barely got a B minus, so who knows."

"That was a killer, though," said Finn. "I'll bet you did great today."

"You're too sweet." Lucy leaned into him and they bumped shoulders.

Forgetting her bizarre behavior, she was right about one thing: Finn was being totally "artificial sweetener"—the kind that makes my teeth ache. Clearly he wanted something. But before I could figure out what that might be, we turned the corner and I forgot all about my brother.

I was too shocked. I'd passed by Second Street a

gazillion times before, but at the moment, I didn't even recognize the place. The entire block had been transformed into a winter wonderland. I'm talking igloos and icicles, twinkling lights and snow people. Like we were in the middle of December—in Alaska. Obviously it was all fake, or at least manufactured. I could hear the hum of three snow machines working overtime.

But the block-long snowstorm wasn't the only thing odd about the scene. All the regular cars parked on the sides of the street were gone, replaced with two crisp rows of silver, futuristic-looking vehicles—something between an army jeep and a semitruck. Except they were propped up by crystal-clear glass so they seemed to float three feet off the ground.

"Does anyone know what this movie is about?" I asked.

"Yeah, I read up on it last night," said Lucy. "It's about a futuristic, post-apocalyptic world where only a handful of teenagers and some grown-up zombies and an army of giant rats have survived, and there aren't enough resources for all three groups, so they're fighting it out, and—oops, my phone is vibrating." Lucy pulled her phone out of her back pocket and read the screen. "Sonya just texted me. She and Beatrix should be right over there." She pointed to a crowd of about twenty people across the street. Beatrix and Sonya saw us and waved.

When we joined them, Sonya said, "Took you long enough!"

I checked my watch. "We came here right when school got out. It's not even four o'clock."

"We've gotta stick to the outside edge so we actually have a chance of being seen on camera," Sonya said.

"And of seeing Seth." Beatrix pointed to one of the trailers parked across the street. "I think that's his dressing room."

"How can you tell which one is his?" I asked, since all six looked identical to me.

"I've seen other people come out of the other five. Plus, it's set back from the street and it's got the most security," she said, and then lowered her voice to a whisper. "Don't look now, but that's the director."

Of course when someone says "don't look now" I have to look, and it's a good thing I did, or I would've missed seeing Jones Reynaldo.

He was tall and skinny with faded black jeans and a matching faded black shirt—like his clothes had spent too much time in the wash. Come to think of it, with his dark, wildly curly hair and his pale skin, it looked like he'd spent too much time in the wash, too—on an extra spin cycle. He wore dark glasses to match the cloudy day.

Jones walked by us quickly and stopped in front of a props person (or at least some guy in a black T-shirt that read "Props" on the back).

"What's your name?" Jones barked.

The props guy was skinny and blond, already nervous looking. But once Jones approached, his shoulders seemed to shrink closer to his chest. "I'm Zander?" he asked, like he wasn't exactly sure.

"Zander who lost the inflatable crowd?" Jones asked.

"Yeah—about that. I'm so sorry. I feel terrible."

"Sorry doesn't bring back a crowd of thirty," barked Jones. "Do you know how hard it's going to be to corral real live extras? And are you the guy who built these snowmen?"

Zander looked behind him, as if hoping Jones were talking to someone else named Zander. "Uh, yeah," he said finally.

"And what were your instructions?" asked Jones.

"To build four large snowmen," said Zander.

"Yes—to build four *large* snowmen," Jones repeated. "Then why, may I ask, are there four pathetically tiny snowmen on this set?"

The guy flinched. "Sorry. I'll fix it."

Jones stalked off. Everything about him reminded me of a playground bully, all grown up.

"He's intense," said Lucy.

"That's one way to put it," I replied.

"I read that they wanted him to direct one of the Harry Potter movies, but he turned them down," Sonya whispered.

"Why?" asked Lucy.

"He doesn't do franchises. That's what he told them, anyway," said Sonya.

"Wow!" I replied. This seemed impressive, although I'm not sure why.

Just then, Jones seemed to notice our crowd for the first time. He began heading our way, until a tall blond woman in a short black dress stepped in front of him. "Reynaldo Jones. Is that you?" she asked.

Jones stopped short in his tracks, flinched with his whole body, and looked up at her. "It's Jones Reynaldo, as I think you know. Just like it was yesterday, Mrs. Weasel. And the day before."

"And I'm Jenna Beasely. Just like I was yesterday, and the day before, and for my whole entire life," said the woman.

So this was my parents' friend. I didn't remember having brunch with her, but she did look vaguely familiar.

"Beasely. Of course. I don't know why I always do that." Jones smirked in a way that said he knew exactly what he was doing.

My friends and I exchanged glances. This was getting interesting.

"What time are you wrapping here?" she asked.

"Impossible to say, since we haven't started shooting." Jones's voice sounded as chilly as the pretend weather. "And I'm sure I don't need to remind you that we have permits to shoot well into the night, and it's only four o'clock now."

"Yes, I'm well aware of your permits," said Jenna. "And of the fact that you violated the terms last night."

"Well, you didn't have to call the police on us," said Jones.

"Actually, I did. And if you go a minute past eight o'clock tonight I'll shut this movie down faster than you can say 'Brooklyn.'"

"Brooklyn!" he shouted.

"Don't test me!" she warned.

"Just kidding. Sheesh. Where's your sense of humor?"

"I'm much funnier when I'm not kept up all night because of some ridiculous movie shoot," she argued.

"It wasn't all night," said Jones. "And we're allowed to work until eleven tonight. We just got an official extension."

"Says who?"

"The mayor's office." Jones smiled smugly, as if daring her to disagree.

Jenna pulled out her cell phone. "I'll call right now to verify that."

Jones held up his hands and trembled in an exaggerated way. "Oooh, she's got a cell phone. How frightening!" he replied sarcastically.

Meanwhile, Jenna punched in the numbers with such force I feared she'd break her phone.

"She's pretty upset," I whispered.

Sonya huffed. "Some people don't appreciate how lucky they are."

Jones stalked off. Jenna went back into her house, which was directly behind the trailer my friends had pointed out earlier.

Soon a woman dressed in black jeans and a red T-shirt approached. She had a giant megaphone and used it even though we stood all of two feet away.

"Will the new inflatable crowd please follow me?" she bellowed.

I raised my eyebrows at my friends.

Sonya shrugged. "At least she said 'please.'"

"Hold it! Stop right there!" the megaphone woman yelled, pointing to our group. "You look like minors."

"We are," Beatrix piped up. "But we have release forms." She collected all of ours and handed over the small stack.

The woman rifled through them, then had everyone walk to the corner of Prospect Park West.

As soon as we got there, Beatrix grabbed my arm and whispered, "Omigosh, that's Brandon Wilson!"

She pointed to a short guy stepping out of the trailer opposite Seth Ryan's.

"Who?" I asked.

"He was in Seth's last two movies. Remember?"

I squinted at the guy. His hair wasn't straight or curly, just puffy. And the color wasn't exactly red or brown, but somewhere in between. He seemed pretty pale, at least from far away. I tried to picture him in a vampire costume. Then dressed as a dog. "Oh, yeah," I said. "How cool!"

"Think we should ask for his autograph?" asked Lucy.

"No way," said my brother.

We watched Brandon talk to Jones and then head back into his trailer.

Then we saw Jones check with Zander on the progress of the snowmen.

Next we watched someone come around and adjust a bunch of lights. I figured they'd need us to do something sometime soon, but everyone ignored us for the next thirty minutes.

"Being an extra involves a lot of standing around," I said to Lucy as someone finally came over and asked us to cross the street. Then we had to stand around there while a group of props people, led by Zander, built new and better snowmen.

Finally, twenty minutes later, Jones barked at us through a megaphone. "Extras—please walk to the end of the block and mill around inconspicuously."

"I don't do a lot of milling," I whispered. "I think I'm going to be conspicuous."

"Shh!" said Beatrix.

We all shuffled over. It's hard to walk in a big crowd, and harder to act natural when you know there are cameras rolling. "Okay, got it. Now go back to where you started and do it again," Jones said. "This time with more feeling."

After doing this same thing six more times, I started worrying about my dogs. They had to be dying to go out. Maybe volunteering to be an extra had been a giant mistake.

I had a lot of homework tonight, too. Not to mention a history test tomorrow, and twenty pages still to read about the Trail of Tears. I didn't know if we'd been standing around for a long time or if it just seemed like that because I was so bored.

I checked my watch. Yup—it had been a long time.

Suddenly, Jones yelled into his megaphone again.

"You! In the green hoodie!" I looked down at my sweatshirt. It was green. I looked around. No one else in the crowd wore a green hoodie. He'd singled me out. But why? I had this feeling like I'd just failed a big test, and the most important information on it was *don't talk*.

But now it was too late. Jones Reynaldo stopped right in front of me.

"Will you stop checking your watch? You're ruining this entire scene. Now we have to shoot all over again."

"I'm so sorry," I said. "It's just—is this going to take much longer?"

"Yes!" he said. "Now get back to your place and stop looking so bored."

I moved back to where I'd been standing, but I could only follow half of his instructions because I'm just not that good of an actor. "Well, um, how much longer?" I asked. I didn't mean to be rude, but I had to know. There were dogs depending on me!

Jones turned around and glared at me. His entire face turned red as he lowered his megaphone and approached. "Who are you?" he asked.

"I'm Maggie Brooklyn Sinclair. It's nice to meet you." I held out my hand. He stared at it like I'd offered him up a rotten fish.

"You think I care?" he huffed.

"Well, you did ask." I put my hands in my sweatshirt pockets. I didn't like this guy.

Now that he stood so close, I saw he had a few pieces

of straw stuck in his hair. Anyone else, I would've told them about it. But Jones? I was afraid to say anything. The guy was seriously angry, and I was seriously intimidated.

"All I meant was, who are you to be interrupting my shoot?"

"Oh," I said. "I guess I'm an extra. But when I signed up I didn't think it would take this long. I only have so much extra time. Ha ha . . . And I'm sort of, well, out of it."

"What are you saying?" he asked.

"That I have to go."

"What?"

I wondered if he was hard of hearing. Maybe I should ask to borrow his megaphone?

"I have to—" I started to repeat myself, speaking louder this time, but he interrupted.

"You can't leave. I'm not finished with my scene. And no one walks off a Jones Reynaldo set."

"But I really have to go."

"Then I'm throwing you off! Quit wasting my time! Get out of here!"

"I'm so sorry," I said, with all sincerity. Yes, this guy was rude; yes, he was a bully, but I didn't want to mess up his movie. I tried to explain. "If I'd known how long this would take when we started, I never would've—"

"Why are you still talking?" he screamed, grabbing his hair. "I said leave. I never want to see you again. Just vanish."

I giggled. I just couldn't help it.

"What's so funny?" he asked.

"You said 'vanish,'" I said. "And your movie is called *Vanished*—right?"

"Right," he said slowly, not quite believing.

"So it's funny, is all."

Jones stared at me like he wanted to strangle me.

Then he threw his clipboard on the ground and stomped on it, reminding me of the last time Beckett's moms told him he couldn't have any more cookies.

Throwing a tantrum over a cookie I could relate to. Especially since one of his moms is such an awesome baker—a pastry chef at one of my and Finn's favorite restaurants. (One that, incidentally, does not serve brunch.)

But this? I didn't know what else to say.

Jones screamed, "You'll never work in this town again!"

This made no sense whatsoever, but it kind of freaked me out. And sometimes when I'm nervous or confused I can't help but laugh.

Unfortunately, this seemed to be one of those times.

I felt the laughter bubble deep in my stomach. It

traveled up into my throat; I couldn't help it. And then it came out.

Yup. I laughed. In Jones Reynaldo's face. Seeing him so irate with all that straw in his hair? The contrast was too much; it just made me laugh harder.

"What's so funny?" he asked.

I tried to explain myself between fits of giggles, but it wasn't easy getting the words out. "Well, I'm actually going to work. You see, I'm a dog walker, and I—"

"I don't care!" he shouted, pulling at his hair with both hands. "Just get out of my face and don't come back. I never want to see you again!"

Well, the feeling was mutual, but I didn't say so. I turned to my friends and said good-bye. Lucy waved. Finn just shook his head—half embarrassed, half trying not to laugh himself.

Beatrix and Sonya backed away like they were afraid to be associated with me. Probably they were worried *they'd* get thrown off the set for just knowing me, and I didn't blame them. I knew how important this was to them, and I didn't want to stand in their way of seeing the amazing Seth Ryan.

If they got to see him, that is.

In truth, we'd been standing out in the fake snow and the real cold for over an hour, and all we'd seen was Jones Reynaldo. And that Brandon guy. And my parents' friend Jenna. And a scared props guy named Zander, and the megaphone lady, and a bunch of other crew members.

As I headed down the street, I noticed something out of the corner of my eye.

In the window of the trailer—the one with all the security guards—someone waved.

His face seemed so familiar. One I'd seen on TV and in movies and in every magazine there is. He was Seth Ryan.

Except the strange part was, he seemed to be waving at me.

"Hey?" I half asked as I waved back, figuring this must be some big misunderstanding. Like, maybe he was merely Seth Ryan's look-alike.

Except when he smiled at me, I knew for sure, because Seth Ryan's smile is unforgettable.

So, that was weird enough, but he seemed to be motioning for me to come closer.

At least it looked that way. I glanced over my shoulder, figuring there must be someone behind me—Jones or another actor or someone else involved in the movie.

But no—this side of the street remained empty.

I turned back around. Not only was Seth still there, he'd also leaned out of his window. "Hey, can you come here for a second?" he asked.

"Sure." I moved closer. "You do mean—"

Except I didn't get to finish my sentence. Because before I knew it, someone grabbed me by the arm and yanked me away.

Chapter 7

. . .

Twenty minutes later, I fished my keys to Isabel's apartment out of my backpack. Through the closed door I heard someone yelling in French.

"*Excusez-moi, où est la salle de bains?*"

Then in English, the same voice asked, "Excuse me. Where is the bathroom?"

French again: "*La salle de bains est au bout du couloir à gauche.*"

And English: "The bathroom is down the hall and to the left."

I wondered whom Isabel had over and why they were so loud.

Then once I stepped inside, I realized the voice came from a French language tape blasting at full volume. Isabel is moving to Paris in a few weeks. Not forever— just for six months. Which is good, because I'd miss her, and I'd especially miss her dog, Preston, my favorite Irish wolfhound, and, coincidentally, the only Irish wolf-hound I know.

Isabel is our landlady. We live three stories above her, and I've known her since forever. She used to be a big Broadway actress. Now she's simply big in every other sense: size, voice, hair, and general presence.

Today her apartment was even messier than usual. There were six old suitcases stacked precariously in the center of her living room, a mountain of clothes piled nearby. Not to mention three overflowing laundry baskets—two filled with laundry and one filled with porcelain cats.

"Isabel?" I called.

"*Est-il va pleuvoir?*" her tape blared. "Is it going to rain?"

People spend too much time talking about the weather, I think. I mean, it's just there, and we can't control it. So what is there to say? Learning how to talk about it in two languages is doubly boring.

"Hello?" I called again. Then I tried, "Ciao?" because maybe she was in a no-English kind of mood. And it did the trick.

When Isabel hurried out of her bedroom, she almost tripped over her long, puffy silver gown. She looked like a giant disco ball; a giant disco ball in purple, fur-trimmed heels that matched her purple-streaked hair. "Maggie! It's been ages!"

She grabbed my shoulders and air-kissed me on both cheeks. Next to both cheeks, I mean.

"I saw you this morning on my way to school," I reminded her.

"I know, but it *feels* as if it's been ages, and I'm practicing the double kiss. I guess I'm just missing you ahead of time. And speaking of time, I've got so much to do, and what time is it? I somehow dropped my watch in the dishwasher and now the face is flooded. Meanwhile, I'm supposed to meet my French tutor at Trois Pommes for macaroons and repartee in twenty minutes. That's French for a cookie and a conversation."

"I figured," I said.

"But I can't leave until I find my other pink flamingo."

"Excuse me?" I asked.

Isabel held up a gigantic pink flamingo lawn ornament. "My other pink flamingo." She said it like it was obvious. "They don't sell these in Paris."

"And this is relevant because . . ."

"Because I rented a lovely garden flat," said Isabel. "And this will fit perfectly, but there's something tacky about having just a single pink flamingo statue."

"I didn't realize that's what made pink flamingos tacky."

Isabel nodded knowingly. "They need to be in pairs. Like shoes and mittens and chocolate truffles—one will simply not suffice."

Sometimes it's best to just let Isabel talk without questioning her logic, especially when one is short on time, which one—I mean *I*—was. I leashed up Preston, who seemed desperate to get out, maybe because he needed a break from the blare of French language tapes. Did I mention how loud they were? And that dogs have extra-sensitive hearing? Poor Preston!

"I'm going to turn this down a little, okay?" I asked, heading to Isabel's ancient and dusty stereo system that was made up of five components, two gigantic speakers, and not even one iPod dock.

Suddenly Isabel looked out her window and clutched her chest. "Oh dear. Maggie, something horrible has happened! My car is gone!"

I rushed to the window and looked at the empty spot in front of our building.

"I must call the police. Now where's my phone? Last time I saw it, I was watching *Glee*." She looked in her potted plant. "I could've sworn I left it right—oh, that's where that went." She picked up her remote control and brushed off some dirt. Then she turned toward the kitchen.

"Didn't you sell it last week?" I asked.

"My phone?" asked Isabel. "Why would I do that?"

"No, your car. You said dealing with parking would be too much of a hassle when you were out of the country. And it's old, and you'd rather just buy a new one when you come home next summer. I had to help you look for the spare keys and registration, remember? They were sewn into your pink satin throw pillow."

"The one that I took from Prince's dressing room!" said Isabel. "Of course. Now I remember. That lovely little landscape designer bought it. And I think he recognized me, too. You know—from my last great production."

I met the guy who bought Isabel's car, and he was maybe twenty years old. Isabel hasn't acted professionally in about that long, but I didn't point this out. Instead I headed for the door with Preston following at my feet. "I'll see you later, okay?"

"*Au revoir!*" Isabel called. "That's French for good-bye."

"Those lessons are really paying off," I said.

"*Oui,*" said Isabel. "That's French for—"

"I think I figured that one out," I called, before closing the door behind me.

I headed in the opposite direction of Second Street, still rattled from earlier this afternoon.

Getting yelled at by a famous movie director had been bad.

Being thrown off the movie set had been worse.

But being accused of stalking Seth Ryan? That's just plain humiliating. And creepy. I'm no stalker. Yet that's exactly what his security guard accused me of being after he grabbed me and literally carried me off the set. I tried explaining to him that *Seth* had been trying to talk to *me*, but even I knew how crazy that sounded. I'm just a regular kid. Seth Ryan is a megastar.

There's no way Seth would want to talk to me. Except he had. But why? Now I'd probably never know.

At least my walk with Preston was uneventful. After I brought him back to Isabel's, I helped her find her oven mitts, her corkscrew, one striped sock puppet, and the red bandanna she wore to her last Springsteen concert. Then I walked the rest of my dogs.

I got home twenty minutes past curfew, but no one seemed to mind. Finn had called to say filming was running late, so he wouldn't make it for dinner. He was going to eat at Lucy's. I guess she was having everyone over after the shoot. I thought about heading there, too, except I hadn't exactly been invited. I stared at the phone and thought about calling Milo again. But what would I say? How was your chess tournament? Guess what—I got accused of being a stalker this afternoon?

I don't think so.

Chapter 8

. . .

I kept forgetting to move the alarm clock to my side of our room, so Finn and I had to run to school again on Thursday. But luckily Ms. Murphy was too distracted to notice us sneak into homeroom late. It's because she was getting everyone ready to embark on our first field trip of the school year.

"Now, if everyone will just get into a single-file line at the door, I'll do attendance in the hallway," she said. We hadn't even left the room and she already seemed stressed out.

"Lucky break," said Finn, joining the line. "Where are we going?"

"Prospect Park, remember?" I asked. "We're meeting up with Cindy Singer, the artist who did the treehouse sculptures. She's giving the entire seventh grade a tour of her work."

"How do you know this?" asked Finn.

"I pay attention," I said. "Plus, Mom got all excited when I asked her to sign the permission slip last week. She's a big Cindy Singer fan. She even tried to get me to read her biography."

"Listen up, everyone," said Ms. Murphy. "I expect you all to be on your best behavior for Ms. Singer. No talking when she's talking. No wandering off. No chewing gum. No texting, no e-mailing, no tweeting, no IM'ing, no 3G-ing. Everyone pays attention. Got it?"

Half the kids looked up from their cell phones to agree.

I thought about raising my hand and asking what 3G-ing even meant, but decided against it.

We joined a few other classes in front of the building, but apparently we were getting tours in shifts and none of my friends were in my group, so I stuck by Finn. Ms. Murphy led us into the park via the Grand Army Plaza entrance, where the artist Cindy Singer waited.

Cindy was tall and skinny with lots of freckles, big black-framed glasses with thick lenses, and a British accent. She was way older than us (obviously), but seemed younger than our parents. "Hello, Fiske Street School students," she bellowed, extending her arms like she wanted to embrace us in a gigantic group hug. "Thank you for coming to see me."

"Like we had a choice!" Finn whispered.

"Shh!" I said.

She pointed to the structure above her—a tree house made out of sticks and suspended about twenty feet in the air. "This is my first installation on this side of the pond," she said, as everyone looked around, confused, since we were nowhere near the pond.

"And by 'pond' I mean, of course, the Atlantic Ocean," Cindy continued, laughing at what I guess was supposed to be a joke. "I live in London, and I've only ever shown my work in Europe until now. And I know what you're all asking yourselves: why would an extremely successful artist bother coming to Brooklyn to show her work? Why not skip this less exciting borough and go straight to Manhattan, which has so many more museums, as well as a rich history of patronage to the arts? Well, I've got two words for you: the monk parakeets."

"Actually, that's three words," said Finn.

I giggled and shushed him.

Cindy cleared her throat. "The monk parakeet is small and green, with gray tufts of feathers around its neck. They are native to Argentina, and back in 1975, someone tried to ship a large crate of them to a pet store in New York City—except the parrots broke out of their crate and flew the proverbial coop. Yes, that's right—they all escaped. And they must've decided that it was too much trouble to fly home to Argentina, so they made their home right here in Brooklyn. That's right—these very exotic South American birds decided to take up residence in Brooklyn, New York."

"I think Dad covered this in that documentary he did on birds," Finn whispered.

"Really?" I asked. "I must've been sleeping through that part."

"It's their quest for freedom and adventure that intrigued me," Cindy went on. "I remember first reading about them in some ornithological book years ago. I've been thinking about them forever, and only just recently came up with the perfect homage to them: human-size tree houses."

She chuckled to herself. And when she noticed the blank stares of our class, she continued. "Anyway, I wanted to give the children of Brooklyn something they don't have. And what better than a tree house? Since most kids in Brooklyn don't have trees in their backyards. Or backyards, for that matter. Or any type of yard."

"So we can really climb up there?" asked Finn.

"Oh, no," Cindy replied, rolling her eyes. "It seems that the city of New York does not agree with my vision. Or at least, the Parks Department didn't want to purchase the insurance necessary to allow these tree houses to be open. So I had to build them without ladders. They are for display purposes only. Shall we continue?" she asked, and then turned and walked farther into the park, not waiting to see if anyone followed.

We all did, staying on the path all the way to Third Street, where we turned left into the Long Meadow.

Cindy stopped when we reached a tall oak tree. Then she turned around and spoke again. "This second piece is made of brick, and installing it was quite the engineering feat. The first tree I selected for the work was not strong enough. But then we found an older, stronger tree, and *voilà*! Here it is."

She pointed up. In a tree, also about twenty feet up, was a small brick house. Four walls, windows on each side, and one door. It seemed heavy and out of place, but in a cool, quirky way.

"This representation is significant because . . ."

As Cindy went on, I tried to pay attention, but often when people talk about art I get a little lost along the way. Or, as was the case this morning, distracted.

I looked around, thinking that if these tree houses *were* in use, they'd be a good hiding place for the dog-egger. Except he or she wouldn't be able to get inside, since Cindy herself said she built them without ladders. Plus, the eggings happened nowhere near these tree houses.

"Does anyone have any questions?" Cindy asked.

Suddenly I felt a sharp jab in my side. Finn had elbowed me, because Cindy was staring straight at me.

I stood tall and nodded, as if I'd been following her all along.

"Yes, dear, what is it?" she asked me.

Oops. My nod was supposed to signify that I'd been paying attention, not that I actually had a question. My stomach fluttered with panic, but luckily Finn jumped in to save me. "How long did this thing take?" he asked.

"About three years to build—from inspiration to installation," Cindy said.

"Interesting that you say three," said Ms. Murphy. "Given what I know about you, I figured there would be three tree houses."

Cindy smiled. "Obviously you're familiar with my work. And there were supposed to be three, but let's just say things didn't work out as I planned. Well, not exactly. And I'm afraid I can't say anything more about that. So thank you for your time, everyone." She gave us a small wave and said, "Ta-ta."

Ms. Murphy thanked Cindy, and we all gave her a round of applause.

"This really was wonderful," said Ms. Murphy. "A true honor and privilege, and you'll be happy to know that the entire seventh grade is going to be writing reports about your life and work."

"That's lovely!" said Cindy, ignoring the groans from my classmates.

I wish I agreed with her. But more than that—I wish I'd paid better attention.

Chapter 9

◆ ◆ ◆

After school and dog walking and a fruitless search for the egger, I was exhausted and starving. When I got home, I found Finn playing video games in the living room. Our apartment was silent except for the bleeps and whirs of his game; something involving a track meet in space.

"Hey," I said.

"Mom and Dad are both working late, but they left us money for pizza," Finn reported.

I sat down next to him. "Want to order?" I asked.

"Nah, let's go out." He turned off the TV, stood up, and stretched. "I need air."

"Where to?" I asked.

"The Pizza Den," he replied like it was obvious, and I guess it should've been. The Pizza Den is one of our favorite hangouts. The pizza isn't exactly delicious, but there are other reasons to go: it's close, it's cheap, and most importantly, pretty much everyone we know goes there.

"Okay, hold on a minute," I said, and quickly headed into our room to change out of my dirty jeans and into some less dirty ones.

As we headed to Seventh Avenue, I asked, "Hey, how come you're home so early, anyway? Doesn't Jones usually keep you longer?"

"Yup, but this afternoon Mom's friend Jenna intervened and accused him of violating child labor laws."

"No way!" I said.

"Way," Finn replied. "Turns out, kids are only allowed to work for a certain amount of hours in a row. And shooting went over the limit last night. Apparently this happens all the time on productions, and if we're not complaining, she shouldn't be—that's what Jones argued, anyway. But Jenna didn't agree. She called the police, and they showed up and stopped the cameras."

"He must've been furious," I said. "Did he throw a huge tantrum?"

"Epic," Finn said with a sly grin. "Jenna was totally ruthless. The woman is completely intent on shutting this production down, by any means necessary."

"That's crazy!" I said.

"It is, in a way," said Finn. "But to be honest with

you, I wouldn't mind if they had to stop. It's been a long, boring two days of standing around."

"I told Lucy not to bother asking you. I still can't believe you volunteered."

Finn shrugged. "So how's the dog-egging case?"

"Terrible! Dogs are being egged every day, and I have no idea who's behind it. The entire thing just seems so random."

"If it weren't for this dumb Seth Ryan movie, I'd totally help," Finn said, pulling out his iPod. "Mind if I listen to music the rest of the way? Red just burned this new album for me, and I haven't had time to listen to it."

He plugged in his earbuds before I could respond, but I didn't mind. It gave me time to think about my case. According to the blogs I'd been reading, three new dogs had been attacked this week: a Saint Bernard, a Yorkie, and a beagle, all near the Ninth Street entrance to the park. I felt like I was missing something obvious, like the answer was out there in the universe and I just wasn't seeing it.

Sometimes when I solve a mystery, the answer will just come to me from nowhere. One second my mind is a blank slate, and in the next, the answer appears, lit up like a neon sign.

But tonight my brain felt more like murky alphabet soup.

Details of the attacks swirled through my brain, making no sense. I didn't even know where to look next.

By the time we got to the Pizza Den, Lucy was waiting outside, standing by the entrance and knitting a tiny dog sweater.

"You can stand and knit at the same time?" asked Finn. "Impressive."

"Cassie ordered three new outfits for Bean and I'm way behind," she said without even looking up from her needles. "Rats! I just lost count of my stitches."

"Sorry," said Finn.

"What are you doing here?" I asked.

"Having dinner with you," said Lucy, tucking the sweater into her bag.

"How did you know I'd be here?"

"Finn told me," said Lucy.

"Really?" I raised my eyebrows at Finn.

He shrugged. "It's no big deal," he said.

They both gave me blank stares, like I was crazy for questioning this development.

"But you don't even like pizza," I said to Lucy.

"I like garlic knots and soda," she replied.

I couldn't argue with her logic, and I didn't even have a chance to, because before I opened my mouth, Finn said, "I invited Milo, too."

"Wait, what?" I asked.

"He asked what we were doing tonight, which seemed

like kind of an obvious hint, so I asked him to come out for pizza, and then I invited Lucy, too."

"So it's like a double date," said Lucy.

"Except none of us is dating," I said.

"Right," said Lucy, with a quick glance to Finn. "I've been meaning to talk to you about that . . ."

"I know you think that I should just ask Milo on a real date, but it's not that easy. And at this point, do I even need to? It's not like we never hang out. We do all the time. And I like how it's really casual—like we just sort of accidentally do something together that might otherwise be classified as a date, but we don't have the pressure because it's not. Except I wish I'd known he was coming tonight because I would've worn something nicer."

"You look great," said Lucy. "And I still don't get why you won't just ask him out."

"Why doesn't he ask me?" I replied.

"He did," said Lucy. "I promise you there is no dog named 'Call me.'"

"I was kidding about that," I told her.

Lucy looked at me with suspicion. "Are you sure?"

"Okay, I was ninety-five percent kidding, but there's always that five percent of risk left over."

Now she rolled her eyes. "This is not a math equation situation. This is your life! And your not calling Milo probably makes him think you're not interested."

"Keep it down!" I said, suddenly worried about who might overhear.

"And how come it's always the guy's responsibility?" asked Finn. "You're the one who's always going on and on about how Mom and Dad have to treat us equally and not fall into gender stereotypes when they ask us to do stuff around the house and that just because you're a girl and I'm a guy does not mean you'll do the dishes while I take out the trash, even though I know for a fact that you hate taking out the trash."

"That's not because I'm a girl," I said. "It's because I hate mice, and ever since I saw that giant one scramble across the street on garbage day I just can't handle it."

"It's true," said Lucy. "This one time I knit a little mouse and I showed your sister and she screamed."

"It looked totally lifelike," I argued.

"That's because of the whiskers," Lucy explained to my brother, throwing her shoulders back proudly. "I made them out of invisible wire."

"You're both missing the point." Finn crossed his arms and leveled his gaze at me. "It's time I told you the truth, Maggie. There's no such thing as a giant mouse."

"You weren't there."

"I didn't have to be. A giant mouse is a rat."

"No!" I gasped.

"Back me up here, Lucy," said Finn.

Lucy shrugged her shoulders sheepishly. "I'm afraid he's right. And look who's coming."

She pointed to Milo walking down the street, and I couldn't help but stare, because Milo does not walk like a regular person. His hands were in his pockets, his head tilted so that his dark hair flopped just perfectly over his big brown eyes in a way that made my heart feel all melty, like the inside of a toasted marshmallow, except not as sticky.

"Hey," I said, once he got closer.

"Hey," he replied.

"Let's eat," said Finn. He opened the door and we all filed inside.

The place was packed. Like, the four of us barely fit inside. Noisy, too.

"How about if Lucy and I save a table," I yelled. "And you guys wait in line."

"Cool," said Milo. "What do you want?"

"I know what she wants," said Finn, clapping Milo on the shoulders. "Lucy, too. Let's go."

"Thanks, Finn," said Lucy, in this super-high voice.

The guys went to the line and Lucy and I wandered around the restaurant looking for a place to sit down, when suddenly I got hit in the face with a breadstick.

"Ouch!" I said, more out of shock than any real pain.

"I'm so sorry," cried a frazzled-looking mom trying to control her twin toddlers.

"It's okay," I said.

"No, it's not." She turned to her daughter. "Now, Bella, you apologize for that. You could've really hurt this poor girl."

Bella wore a purple tutu, a smudge of pizza sauce on her face, and a look of stubborn indignation. She crossed her arms, looked from me to her mom, and pouted.

"We do not throw things," her mother said.

"Yes we do," Bella replied.

Her mom blinked and took a deep breath. "Bella, say you're sorry, now."

Bella stomped her foot.

"If you don't apologize now, we're leaving."

Lucy and I looked at each other, both of us thinking the same thing: *Please don't apologize, Bella. Not if it means you'll be giving up this great table. Stick to your guns!*

Bella picked up her cup of water, dumped it on the floor, then climbed on top of the table and began tap dancing.

Her mom scooped up Bella and her brother and deposited them in a large double stroller. Lucy and I swooped in before she could finish buckling them down.

"Yes!" said Lucy as we bumped fists.

"Sweet!" I replied. "Those toddlers are like ticking time bombs."

"Lucky for us." Lucy giggled. "So, Finn told you the movie got shut down early tonight, right?"

"I heard all about it. Are Sonya and Beatrix disappointed?"

"They both are, but I'm kind of relieved. Being an extra is much less glamorous than I imagined. It's like we're just this big herd of cattle that gets shuffled from one side of the sidewalk to the other. All we do is stand around and wait. We've hardly seen a glimpse of Seth Ryan. I think that bugs them more than anything."

"Maybe that's for the best," I said, still pretty upset about my run-in with his security guard—something Lucy knew all about.

"Yeah, but Seth is the only reason we all signed up to be extras. Beatrix and Sonya tried to get close to ask for his autograph for their scrapbook, but this lady with big blond hair came over and started yelling at them. So they ran away."

"That's not cool, but better to be run off than carried off."

"Too true." Lucy sighed. "Still, sometimes I wish the inflatable crowd had never blown away. You're kind of lucky you got thrown off the set."

"Except once the movie comes out I'll be totally jealous that you guys are going to be in it. Plus, I got accused of being a stalker, which could not be more humiliating."

"There's that," said Lucy. "Hey, I have to run to the bathroom. You okay holding this table solo?"

"Sure," I replied, glancing at Finn and Milo. The line snaked almost to the door, and they were still practically at the end of it.

Just then Milo caught my eye and waved.

I waved back, wondering if maybe he thought this was a date. Was he going to walk me home after? Would we hold hands? Should I try to kiss him?

Soon after Lucy left, this teenage couple swooped in like vultures and asked if I was leaving. "Nope. Just waiting for my friends," I said.

After they moved on, a mom with a newborn attached to her chest asked me if I'd mind if she changed her baby on the tabletop, and I said, "Ew, no. I mean, yes, I do mind."

And then some guy came over and asked if he could sit down.

I'd definitely heard his voice somewhere before. But I couldn't place him. Not right away, with his face obscured by a big blue baseball cap. It was pulled down low and his shoulders were hunched like he was trying to shrink into himself.

I said, "Sorry, dude. Table's taken."

But he continued standing, grinning this goofy, nervous, and kind of familiar grin.

I gave him a closer look and realized I *had* seen him before—many times.

And he wasn't just some guy.

He was Seth Ryan.

Chapter 10

. . .

"Hey, can I ask you something?" Seth wondered, all casual. Not just like we knew each other—more like we were best buds who hung out all the time and it was perfectly normal for us to meet up for pizza on a Thursday night. He acted like he didn't even remember his security guard bombarding me yesterday.

And I know he's this super celebrity who can make millions of hearts race all across the universe with one famous on-screen smile, but seeing him up close in real life after yesterday? Even though half of me wanted to do giddy backflips of joy, I snapped.

"Not until I ask you something," I said. "What's the deal with calling me over to your trailer and then disappearing when your security guard shows up?"

Seth blinked and straightened up, truly stunned. Maybe because I yelled at him. Yes, probably because of that. I didn't mean to. Honestly, it just sort of happened.

And I could see how he's not used to people raising their voices at him. With the exception of screaming fans, I mean.

But I didn't expect him to look so scared. He stood there frozen. I'm talking full-on statue pose. I could have knocked him over with a finger. Which meant I'd just scared the most famous guy in Hollywood— something I now felt bad about.

"You okay?" I asked.

"No. I mean, yes, I'm fine. And I'm sorry." Seth blinked and readjusted his baseball cap, sort of straightening it—not because it needed to be straightened, but because he needed something to do. "You're right. It's just—I don't know. Sorry to bug you . . ." He backed away—or tried to, that is, but instead he walked straight into someone's giant red baby stroller.

"Watch it!" yelled the baby's dad. "You're jostling my Guthrie."

Heads swiveled as every parent in the entire restaurant turned to look at Seth.

"Sorry!" Seth said, raising his hands up in surrender.

"*SSSHHH!*" Guthrie's dad raised his finger to his lips. "Keep it down, pretty boy!"

Seth seemed taken aback, even more startled than before.

I kept waiting for someone to recognize him and ask for an autograph. But no one did. Then I realized why:

Seth is huge with kids my age, but most grown-ups wouldn't recognize him. Tonight's crowd was too old and too young at the same time. The Pizza Den is a huge after-school hangout, but I guess everything shifts at night—this crowd was pretty much all grown-ups and babies, with the exception of me and Finn and company.

And one superstar whose appearance still confused me in a major way.

Seth tried to make for the door but stopped short, balancing on his heels to avoid bumping into the triplets in high chairs blocking his path. He seemed afraid to get too close, not that I could blame him, considering he was trapped in the Park Slope web. The guy needed serious help.

"Here, sit down." I tugged on the sleeve of his jacket. "I'm sorry. I didn't mean to yell."

He hesitated. "You sure?"

"Positive."

He sat down, relieved. "Thanks. Oh, I'm Seth Ryan, by the way. You're Maggie, right?"

"Yes, Maggie Brooklyn," I replied.

"Brooklyn? You mean like where we are right now?" asked Seth.

"Yes, exactly that," I replied.

Seth scratched his neck. "Why did your parents name you after a state?"

"Um, Brooklyn isn't a state. It's a borough of New York City," I said, correcting him.

"A what?" asked Seth.

"New York City," I repeated.

"Oh, right. Of course." Seth held out his hand. "Nice to meet you, Maggie Borough. I'm sorry about what happened this afternoon. I told Vigor he went a little overboard, but everything happened so fast, I didn't know what to do. And he was only trying to protect me."

Seth's handshake was firm—all business, like we were signing a deal. It was a funny contrast to his appearance. What I'd first mistaken for a necklace was actually the tag on Seth's T-shirt. He wore it inside out and backward. He also had on sweatpants with one leg tucked into his sock.

"Um, nice to meet you, too?" I don't know why my voice got so high at the end of my sentence, like I had doubt when I did not. It was nice to meet him. No question.

Except for all my questions about why *he* wanted to meet *me*.

I waited, and he smiled his movie-star smile. Warm, inviting, and totally sincere. Also, mesmerizing—despite the goofy wardrobe.

I got lost in that smile for a minute. "So can I?" he asked.

"Can you what?"

"Talk to you."

"Yes, of course," I said. "I mean, sure, if you want to. My friends will be back in a minute, but you could totally join us." I looked toward the line. Finn and Milo were still pretty far back. Now Lucy had joined them, and she and Finn were pelting each other with red plastic straws. No one looked my way. Not even after I waved to try to get their attention.

"I know you're busy, so I'll only stay for a minute," he said, taking a deep breath. "But the reason I noticed you on set the other day is because I saw the way you talked to Jones."

I cringed and buried my head in my hands. "I'm so sorry about that. I didn't mean to mess up your movie or anything. I really wanted to be an extra. It's just—I had to go, and he didn't get that."

"I know—I heard the whole thing," he said, leaning a bit closer. "And I'm wondering—how did you do it?"

"How did I do what?"

"You know—stand up to him. How come you weren't intimidated? Most people are scared of Jones."

"I can kind of see why, since he's got that whole screaming-his-head-off thing mastered, but it's just something I had to do. I didn't even think about it."

Seth shook his head, seemingly amazed. "I could never have done that."

"Wait—you're kidding, right?"

"No way."

"But you're Seth Ryan."

"Exactly. I'm Seth Ryan, and I always do what I'm supposed to do. Fiona tells me it's the secret to my success, and I shouldn't overthink things because my brain will hurt and it'll cause stress and worry lines, and I can't afford worry lines. They'll show up on camera—especially with all this new high-definition technology."

"Who's Fiona?" I asked, figuring it was his new girlfriend.

"Fiona is my manager. She kind of discovered me, and she totally knows what's best for me. And what's best is knowing one thing: never question your director. He or she is boss." Seth nodded once, agreeing with his own point. He sounded like a robot—totally programmed.

"I see," I said slowly, even though I didn't. Not when Jones Reynaldo, Seth's current boss, acted like a spoiled toddler—and even worse than the tap-dancing toddler from just a few minutes ago.

He squinted at me. "So what was so important that you had to leave?"

"My dogs," I replied. "Well, not *my* dogs exactly. They're my clients; I'm a dog walker."

"A what?" asked Seth.

"I walk a bunch of dogs. It's my after-school job."

Seth gave me a blank look, like he'd never heard of a dog walker, so I explained further. "Basically, I pick them up after school, get them outside so they can have fresh air and exercise and relieve themselves, and take them home again. Some of them like to play fetch, too."

"That sounds like the coolest job in the world," Seth marveled.

"Are you making fun of me?" I asked, just to be sure.

"No way. I'm serious. I think that's awesome. I love dogs. I've always wanted one."

I stared at him for a few moments, still not completely convinced this wasn't an elaborate prank. Like, maybe there was a hidden camera somewhere. It just seemed too weird that this megastar would be hanging out with me at the Pizza Den.

"So why don't you get one?" I asked. "It's not like they're so expensive. You can buy ten dogs, or maybe ten thousand. Isn't it true that you have seven cars? One for each day of the week?"

"To be honest, I don't know," said Seth. "My manager handles all that stuff. I can't even drive. I have a lot of investments, I guess. I know there's a loft in SoHo. I was there once, but it seemed kind of empty." Suddenly his face lit up. "Oh, but I saw pictures of it in *Teen People* last month and it looked awesome, so I guess someone furnished it."

"You mean you're not staying there?"

Seth looked at me like I was crazy. "We are in Brooklyn. You know that, right, Maggie?"

I laughed. "Hello? Brooklyn is my middle name—literally. So I'm pretty positive that Brooklyn is close to Manhattan. Like I said before, it's still considered New York City."

"Oh." Seth paused and frowned. "I thought you were kidding about that."

"Nope. There are five boroughs in this city." I ticked them off on my fingers. "Manhattan, Brooklyn, Queens, the Bronx, and Staten Island."

He leaned back and grinned. "Now you're just messing with me."

Was he serious? He seemed to be, but how was that even possible?

"You know that Manhattan is just over the bridge? And SoHo is probably less than five miles away," I said.

Seth's smile faded, which told me he hadn't been joking—and now I'd embarrassed him. He coughed. "Well, geography was never my best subject. Not that I'm in school anymore. I have my own tutor and I always get straight As. In fact, I just finished the ninth grade—two whole years early."

"Really?" I asked, more than a little surprised.

Because it seemed like basic geography was something Seth's tutor should've covered before giving him any sort of degree. But what did I know? I mean, besides the five boroughs of the city. Okay, I knew a lot, but I'm sure Seth did, too. He had to be smart, because acting is hard.

I know, because my mom signed Finn and me up for drama camp one summer when we were nine. Memorizing lines was difficult enough, but more challenging than that was getting to know characters inside and out and then communicating that to the audience through a performance. It took brains and hard work and discipline and talent and guts. Seth had all that. I could just tell.

Still, the geography thing was weird.

"Fiona probably has us staying out here because it's safer," Seth reasoned. "More convenient, too. Our hotel is just a few blocks away, although I'm not supposed to tell anyone that. Anyway, about the dog: she says I can't have one because it would get in the way of my work. And I'm always traveling and my hours are crazy, so it's not like I even have time to take care of one. I mean, I guess I could hire a dog walker, but that doesn't make sense because I'm always shooting in different locations. Like, we're only here in Brooklyn for a few more days and then we're heading to Toronto, which is cool because I love Europe."

"Um, Toronto is in Canada," I said.

"Yeah," said Seth. "I know."

"Which is technically North America. You can even drive there from here."

Seth blinked. "Are you sure? Because everyone told me it was European."

"I'm positive," I said.

"Are you some kind of genius?" asked Seth.

"I'm just a regular kid," I promised. "Anyway, you must take breaks. Go home sometime."

"Home?" Seth tilted his head, confused.

I had to smile. "You must come from somewhere . . ."

"Oh, yeah." He took off his baseball cap for a second and pushed his bangs away from his forehead. "I was born in Buffalo. It's upstate."

"Is that where your family is?" I asked.

"It's just me and my dad. I mean, it *was* just me and my dad, but not anymore."

"I'm so sorry!" I said.

"Oh, he's not dead," said Seth. "He's just not around. It's kind of complicated."

Seth seemed like he didn't want to talk about his dad, so I didn't push it, although I was curious. "It must be hard, being so far away from him."

Seth didn't answer me directly. In fact, he seemed kind of uncomfortable, so I decided to change the subject. I told Seth about how I couldn't have a dog, either. "It's because my brother is allergic. Which is annoying, but if I had my own dog I probably never would've started walking other people's dogs. So actually I'm lucky."

"I'm jealous," said Seth.

I laughed, figuring he was kidding. "Being a dog walker is hardly something to envy. Anyone could do it."

Seth shook his head. "I don't think so. I wish I had a cool job like yours."

"Um, you're a movie star. Like, world famous. Tons of people would kill to do that," I reminded him.

"Yeah, that's the problem," said Seth. He picked up the pepper and spilled some out on the table, then traced one finger through the grains. "Fiona says I shouldn't trust anyone, and she's right. But I don't know. . . . Sometimes it's kind of lonely." Suddenly he looked up at me. "Do you ever wish you could just, like, walk away from your life?"

I was taken aback. Kind of a profound question for a Thursday night. "Um, what do you mean?"

"I don't know—do you ever wish things had turned out differently?"

"Well, sure," I replied. "All the time. But it's not like my life is over. Things change constantly."

Seth sighed. "Maybe for you; but for me it's always the same. Yeah, there are different movies in different cities, but it's always the same story." He sounded so resigned, so dreary; this real Seth Ryan was so different from the cool, easy-going star I thought I knew. I had a million questions for him, but before I could figure out what to ask first, a tiny woman with big blond hair stormed into the Pizza Den and headed straight for our table.

She sat down next to Seth and asked, "Where have you been? Do you know how worried I was?"

Seth didn't answer, but he seemed to shrink three whole inches, right before my eyes.

"You can't pull stunts like this!" she said, then whipped her head around to face me. "And you can't hound him like this. Seth is very nice to his fans, but even he has his limits. If you want an autograph, you'll have to write to the studio. Or come to his book signing next month. He'll be at the Barnes and Noble in Union Square."

"Who are you?" I asked.

"I'm Fiona Stern," she replied. "Seth's manager."

"Wait, I'm writing a book?" asked Seth.

Fiona ruffled his hair. "No, sweetie, you already did."

"I did?" asked Seth, thoroughly confused. "Because I think I'd remember."

Fiona raised her finger to her lips and shushed him. "Just stop talking and keep smiling," she said, turning to me. "My point is that Seth doesn't have time for such nonsense, and he can't afford to damage his hands."

"I never asked for an autograph," I argued. "I was just sitting here, and he—"

"And Seth Ryan is a minor. I don't know what you think you're doing or what you want, but I won't have it."

"I'm a minor, too," I said. "Younger than Seth, even."

Fiona held up her hand. "Just leave him alone."

Seth looked down at his lap. I could barely see his face under his baseball cap, but something told me it was bright red. I kept waiting for him to stand up for me, to tell this woman that he's the one who started our conversation, but he didn't. Kind of like the scene with the bodyguard. Although this time, I could see him wimp out close up.

Which annoyed me—yet at the same time, made me feel sorry for the guy.

And just then, Finn and Milo and Lucy walked back with all of our food. "What's going on?" asked Lucy. She stared from me to Seth. "Did anyone ever tell you that you look just like Seth—"

Fiona grabbed her arm before she could finish.

"Yee-ouch!" Lucy yelled.

"Keep quiet and do not say his name so loud," Fiona hissed. Then she turned to Seth. "Have you already forgotten about the riot in Pittsburgh?"

"Yeah, sorry," Seth whispered, his voice kind of shaky.

This seemed to anger Fiona even more. "What are you doing here, anyway? This place is disgusting." Suddenly she turned to me. "You haven't fed him any pizza, have you? *Vanished* takes place in Norzenia—a future, post-apocalyptic world with a very low food supply, so Seth needs to keep his weight down. Kids are skinnier there. They don't get to go out for pizza whenever they want to. Know why? Because all the pizza joints burned down after the gargantuan atomic fireball. Seth has been on a very strict diet for months, and I'd hate to see him ruin it. And this place does not look so clean." She turned to Seth and said, "We're checking your clothes for bedbugs as soon as we get back to the hotel."

She looked him up and down, seemingly taking in his outfit for the very first time. "Oh, sweetie. I can't believe you left your room like that. You look awful. On second thought, we'll just burn the clothes."

"The Pizza Den is great," I said, even though I didn't really believe it.

"Maybe for you," said Fiona.

I turned to Seth, waiting for him to stand up for himself at the very least, but he kept the frozen zombie grin on his face. Clearly the guy just didn't know what to do.

"Seth?" I asked, trying one last time.

Finally he snapped out of it and mumbled, "Sorry."

But he said it to the ground, so I couldn't tell if he was apologizing to me or to Fiona.

Then he pulled his baseball cap down even farther.

"We need to go—now!" Fiona tried to pull him away, but Seth dodged her grasp.

"Hey, you should come see me tomorrow," Seth said to me.

"I'm not allowed to, remember? Jones banned me from the set."

Seth gave me a half grin. "I know, but I'm not talking about the—"

Fiona huffed. "Let's go. This isn't safe." With a final withering glare at me, she grabbed Seth by the arm and whisked him away.

Chapter 11

. . .

"Who was that?" asked Milo, setting his plate of mozzarella sticks and ginger ale on the table.

I groaned. "Seth's manager, Fiona. She's pretty awful, huh?"

"No, I mean the dude with his pant leg tucked into his sock. He doesn't live around here, does he?"

I blinked at Milo, trying to figure out if he was kidding. Somehow, he didn't seem to be. But how was that even possible?

Lucy slapped her palm down on the table, rattling both us and all of our plastic-ware. "Are you telling us you didn't recognize Seth Ryan just now?" she asked.

"Seth who?" Milo replied, completely confused.

"Dude, either you're joking or you're seriously out of the loop," said Finn.

Milo pointed over his shoulder toward the door.

"Is that the actor everyone in school's been talking about?"

"Yes," I replied. "He's that actor."

"Did he yell at you again for messing up his movie? Because I'm happy to go after him." Milo was already half out of his seat. A nice gesture, but also a strange one.

"No, no, no. That was the director who yelled— Jones Reynaldo. Seth is a total sweetheart," I explained. "We were just talking."

No one said anything, because they were too busy gaping at me.

"What?" I asked.

"Sweetheart?" asked my brother.

I shrugged. "He was."

Finn shook his head like I'd said something crazy.

Milo kind of smirked, but I don't know why.

Lucy leaned closer and said, "I can't believe you were just hanging out with Seth Ryan. That's beyond amazing!"

I giggled and felt my face heat up. "I know. So crazy, right?" It had seemed strange enough in the moment, but now that it was over, it really hit me—Seth Ryan had been wandering around the neighborhood looking for me.

I'm glad we were sitting, because my knees felt

wobbly, like when our entire social studies class took the Circle Line cruise around the Statue of Liberty last year. There hadn't been enough seats for everyone, so I'd had to stand for over an hour. When we got off the boat, I still felt like I was at sea, even hours later.

That's how I felt now, like I'd just gotten off the boat. Except Seth Ryan was, in many ways, a lot more spectacular than Lady Liberty. If I had to stand up right now, I'd need to steady myself on the back of the booth. But luckily, I didn't.

"So what's he like?" Lucy asked. "Tell me everything!"

"Um, there's not much to tell," I replied. I didn't mean to come off as coy. I had nothing to hide. I just didn't know what to say, since I was still trying to figure out what happened, and why Seth had sought me out.

Was he really impressed with how I'd stood up to Jones Reynaldo?

Did he really always do what he was told to without question?

Were all famous people that bad at geography?

"Did you get a picture with him?" asked Lucy. "Tell me you got a picture with him!"

"It's not like I carry around my camera," I replied. "And I'm still saving up for a cell phone." Finn and I are the only kids we know, practically, who don't have them.

"Well, what about an autograph?" asked Lucy.

"It didn't really come up."

Lucy slapped her palm against her forehead. "How could you not ask for his autograph?"

"Did he have a really big head?" Milo interrupted.

"Not at all—he was super modest," I said. "Totally mellow, too. He's not at all what I expected—especially after being screamed at by Jones Reynaldo. I figured everyone in Hollywood was super sensitive and short tempered but Seth Ryan . . . he's different."

"No," said Milo. "I'm talking literally. His head seemed way oversize."

"Sonya and Beatrix are going to freak!" said Lucy. "How did you do it?"

"Do what?"

"Approach him."

"I didn't," I said. "He came over to me and asked to sit down. He said he'd been looking for me."

"Omigosh!" said Lucy. "He likes you."

"He does not like me," I said, so loud I surprised myself, and Milo, too, who stared at me, alarmed. "He just wanted to talk about—"

Milo interrupted. "I think he was wearing makeup."

"All actors wear makeup," I said. "It's just part of the job."

"I could never be an actor, then," said Milo. He tried

balancing the saltshaker on top of the pepper shaker, but it toppled over almost instantly.

I tried to catch his eye, but he wouldn't look at me. Not like he didn't notice, more like he was purposely avoiding me.

Finn laughed and asked, "What's wrong with makeup? Does it threaten your masculinity?"

"No way, dude. The problem is, my skin's too sensitive. I'd break out in a second," Milo replied, finally pushing the salt and pepper aside.

Lucy burst out laughing, and I couldn't help but join in.

"What?" asked Milo. "It's true. This one time I accidentally got sprayed by one of those perfume ladies at the mall. I think she was aiming for my grandma; anyway, five minutes later I had hives the size of quarters all over my body."

"Perfume isn't makeup," I said.

"Well then, what is it?" asked Milo.

"I don't know. A scent?"

"A scent you can buy wherever makeup is sold," Milo pointed out.

"Right, but that doesn't mean it's makeup. Shampoo and conditioner and soap are all sold in the same aisle at the grocery store, but that doesn't mean they're the same thing."

"They're all soap," said Milo. "And perfume and lip-stick are both beautifying products."

At that, all three of us cracked up. We just couldn't help ourselves.

"What?" asked Milo, totally offended.

"It's nothing personal," I said. "It's just funny to hear you say 'beautifying products.' "

"Well, that's exactly what they are," he argued.

"Sorry," I said. "You're right. I didn't mean to laugh, and it doesn't matter that you've never heard of Seth Ryan. You should see one of his movies sometime, though. Um, maybe we can rent one this weekend."

I almost didn't say that last part. Asking Milo out on a real date was hard enough. But doing so in front of an audience? I couldn't believe I'd actually gotten the words out.

Lucy shot me a secret thumbs-up—embarrassing, but sweet, and exactly what I needed. I grinned and looked away, realizing she was right. It was time to stop this wimpy waiting, time to step up. It's hard for guys to put themselves out there. And Milo had with that note. Which I'd pretty much ignored up until this moment. (At least as far as he was concerned; he had no idea how many times I'd read it and attempted to analyze his handwriting for some deeper meaning.) I was feeling pretty good now that I'd finally done it.

At least until Milo opened his mouth. "Forget it. I'm busy. Anyway, I don't think I could get over his big head."

Yikes.

No, better make that double-yikes.

I looked at Lucy, who cringed down at her half-empty plate.

"Food's getting cold. Let's eat," said Finn, who hadn't bothered waiting for us anyway. He was already on his second piece. But I was glad he said something.

Lucy grabbed a garlic knot and ripped off a large chunk with her teeth. "Delicious," she said with her mouth full—clearly trying to deflect my own personal moment of humiliation.

I'd lost my appetite, but bit into my slice of pepperoni anyway, just to have something to do. It was cold and greasy. Which pretty much fit my mood.

I didn't want to look at Milo, but couldn't help noticing him eating his mozzarella sticks out of the corner of my eye. Sulkily.

"Have you guys started your report on Cindy Singer?" asked Lucy.

"That artist lady?" asked Finn.

"I think the technical term for a female artist is simply 'artist,'" I said.

Finn threw his crust at me. "If she were a dude, I'd have said 'artist dude.'"

"No food fighting," said Lucy. "We cannot go there!"

"Sorry," said Finn.

"It's okay," I replied, removing the crust from my lap and putting it on my tray.

"Anyway," said Lucy, "I just read about this exhibit she had last year in London. She created this whole Hansel and Gretel–themed candy house, and it was life-size and made out of real gingerbread and gumdrops. It was on display at the Serpentine Gallery in Hyde Park, and one morning when they opened up, one of the sides had collapsed. At first they thought it was vandals or maybe art thieves or something. But once they took a closer look, they realized it was ants. Like, thousands of them—they actually ate the exhibit!"

"That's wild, but not totally surprising," said Finn. "Ants are insanely strong—they can carry objects that are fifty times their body weight with their mandibles. And they've been around since the dinosaurs."

"Really?" asked Lucy, wide-eyed and—in my opinion—overly impressed.

So my brother did a study of ants for his most recent science report and he happened to retain the information. Guess what—I could spout off plenty of facts about wolves: they're the largest members of the dog family. They can roam up to twelve miles in a single day, and they can eat twenty pounds of meat in a single sitting. But I didn't need to share any of this, because I didn't need to show off.

Not that Milo would have been impressed by anything I had to say at the moment.

We both picked at our pizza in silence while Finn and Lucy talked.

Ten minutes later when they finally took a break, I said, "I should get home. It's late."

I'd never seen Milo stand up faster. "Me, too. See ya around," he said before bolting for the door.

Once he was gone, I turned to Lucy and Finn. " 'Just ask him out. He's shy.' Great idea. Not!"

Lucy and Finn both gave me looks of sympathy, which just made me feel worse.

"Sorry, Maggie," said Lucy.

"I don't know what I did, but obviously he hates me," I replied as we gathered up our trash.

"He doesn't hate you," said Lucy. "He's just in a weird mood, I guess. I don't know. Maybe he's upset that we laughed at his whole makeup-allergy thing."

"I didn't mean to laugh," I said. " 'Beautifying products' sounds really funny. Try saying it without laughing."

Lucy said, "Beautify," and struggled to maintain a straight face, which just set us both off laughing again.

"Dude, give the guy a break and let it go. Anyway,

that's not it," Finn said, standing up and chucking his soda into the trash can. "You're both missing the obvious. The guy is jealous!"

"Of what?" I wondered.

"Of Seth Ryan," Finn said to me. "Because he thinks you're crushing on the guy!"

Chapter 12

. . .

I couldn't sleep that night. And not just because I felt slightly sick from my pizza—I'm used to that. My problem was boys—as in, Seth and Milo.

My conversation with Seth Ryan seemed so odd, so out of the blue. I'm glad my friends saw me talking to him. Otherwise by now I'd probably have convinced myself I made the whole thing up. On the other hand, if I had made up our encounter, I wouldn't even be able to invent a character like Seth Ryan. He was nothing like the guy I'd imagined.

In every single movie he starred in, Seth came across as a brilliant mastermind—the kind of guy who always knew what to say and what to do, whether that meant thwarting a gang of giant lobsters or defending the planet from a madman by disarming a gigantic ticking time bomb with half a toothpick and only seconds to spare.

And it wasn't just the roles he played; even in interviews, Seth seemed cool and happy and completely together. From seeing his image on TV and his pictures in magazines, I'd figured he had an amazing fashion sense.

But Seth in real life? He reminded me of a brand-new puppy set loose in the park. He didn't know where he was, how to act, what to do, or which way was up. Also, and this part made me sad, he seemed completely lost and alone.

I'm not the best-dressed kid in the world, but at least I knew how to put my T-shirts on the right way. Unless wearing his T-shirt inside out and backward was some sort of new trend I hadn't heard about yet. Somehow, I didn't think so.

And how come Seth let Fiona boss him around like that? Shouldn't he be able to take a walk and grab a slice of pizza when he wanted to? He's twelve, not two. It didn't make any sense. If he really wanted a dog, why didn't he just go out and get a dog? What Fiona said about him working too much kind of made sense. But why couldn't he take some time off? As far as I knew, he'd been working his whole life. Everybody deserved a vacation.

The more I thought about our encounter, the less sense it made. And the less sense it made, the more my head hurt.

Then there was Milo, who'd not only acted like a total jerk, he'd also acted like a weird jerk. Was Finn right? Was he jealous of Seth Ryan? That sounded silly. Maybe he was really mad at me for something else. But why would he be mad? I didn't do anything wrong. And it's not like I wanted Seth to be my boyfriend. But even if I did, so what? Milo and I weren't officially together.

I tossed and turned in my bed, too worked up to sleep, and now annoyed with Milo for being mysteriously annoyed with me.

Unless something else was going on with Milo. Maybe he was nervous about his upcoming chess tournament, or stressed out about school, or fighting with his grandma. It could've been a million things. By the time I went to sleep, I'd convinced myself it wasn't about me. I must've misinterpreted his silence. Maybe he really was busy all weekend. I had bigger things to worry about: a report on Cindy Singer and an egger to track down.

But when I got to science the next day and said hi to Milo, he didn't respond. At first I figured he hadn't heard. He wasn't listening to music, but he was bent over a book. Some science fiction novel, I guessed, based on the cover. Milo reads them all the time.

"Good book?" I asked, raising my voice.

"Huh?" He turned around. "Oh, hey," he said.

"I've been thinking about Mister Fru Fru's egger

and I'm wondering if he or she could be a cat owner. Like, maybe someone really upset with how Park Slope is overrun with dogs?"

I was half joking. Really, I just wanted to have a conversation, make things normal again. But Milo didn't even smile.

Chapter 13

◆ ◆ ◆

I took Preston on an extra-long walk after school that day because walking helps me think, and I had a lot of thinking to do.

Maybe Milo was mad because Lucy and I had laughed at his beautifying products comment. So should I apologize? What if that wasn't it? And even if it was—what if bringing it up now, a day later, made everything even worse? And how could I waste so much time worrying about it when I had a dog-egger to catch?

Unless Finn was right and Milo did like me and now I'd blown our entire relationship before we even had a chance to have one.

Wandering around the park did not bring any clarity to the situation.

I decided to swing by the set of *Vanished*. Yes, Jones had banned me, but Seth and I were friends. Okay, maybe not friends, but we were certainly friendly, and he'd told me to stop by.

Rounding the corner from Prospect Park West onto Second Street, I expected to see the crazy winter wonderland I'd encountered on Wednesday. But Zander and the rest of the crew must've been working overtime, because today the street looked like a genuine crime scene.

Each of the six trailers was cordoned off with yellow police tape that read CRIME SCENE DO NOT CROSS in bold black letters. A bunch of men and women in New York Police Department uniforms wandered around.

They looked so serious, and had authentic-looking caps and everything. But according to Beatrix and Sonya, *Vanished* took place in a universe overrun by teenagers and zombies and giant rats. So why the fake cops? Were they supposed to be teenage cops? These ones seemed too old. Maybe they were zombie cops? They weren't particularly pale, and everyone knows that if the walking dead are one thing, it's pale. The cameras weren't rolling, but some of them talked into walkie-talkies. Others marched around like they meant business. In other words, they looked like real, live cops. And I had this funny feeling, like something major had gone down.

I looked for my friends, thinking maybe they could tell me why the police were there. But before I found them, I noticed a familiar face.

It was one of the police officers who'd helped me when I busted the dog-napper last month. He stood off to the side, half hidden by one of the larger brownstones on the street, talking into his cell phone. I walked Preston closer so I could listen. Okay, eavesdrop. I couldn't help but be curious. "He didn't show up for work this morning, and his hotel room was empty. Dressing room, too," the officer said. "His manager and legal guardian. Negative. No sign of a break-in or struggle. We've got to talk to the director, too. I know. Yeah, we have no choice. The note on the bed, that's all it said. 'Don't bother looking, you'll never—' "

Just then he stopped talking and glanced at me.

I quickly crouched down to pet Preston. "How ya doing, big guy? Ready to move on?" I spoke in that overly friendly tone people use when talking to dogs and children. And I did my best to look the part of an innocent kid walking her dog—which I realize is not too much of a stretch. The police officer must have believed me, because he went on talking, although in a much lower voice.

Now I had to strain to make out the words.

". . . Could be anyone . . . Not just a kid—the most famous kid in the world."

Suddenly my ears perked up. Obviously there's only one most famous kid in the world: Seth Ryan. But did the police officer just say something about a ransom note? That didn't sound good. I looked up at him right as he looked at me. Our eyes met, which meant one thing—I was busted.

He hung up and pointed to me in one swift move. "I know you," he said.

I flashed him my most innocent look. "Are you talking to me?" I asked.

"You're the kid who saved all those dogs last month, right? Maggie Brooklyn Sinclair, is it?"

"You can call me Maggie Brooklyn."

"I never got to introduce myself last time. I'm Officer Rudy Green, but you can call me Rudy. I'm impressed with your work. Brenda had been stealing dogs for years, all over the country. Every other detective was looking for a set of twins. No one realized she was a lone operator."

"It took a while to figure out," I admitted, going for a modest approach.

I shook his hand, which was large, like the rest of him. Rudy Green had dark skin and brown eyes. Tall and skinny, he wore his police cap back a bit on his shaved head.

"Is everything okay?" I asked. "I couldn't help but overhear . . ."

"Nothing you need to worry about," he said.

Too late for that. I looked around. A few more police

cars pulled up. A lady in a dark gray suit took pictures of Seth's trailer. A group of officers talked to Vigor, Seth's bodyguard. Others seemed to be questioning Jones and various members of the cast and crew. The air felt tense, too serious. And someone was conspicuously missing.

"Where's Seth?" I asked, more than a little concerned.

Rudy smiled a tight smile. "You two on a first-name basis?"

"Um, yeah," I said. "We are. Is he okay?"

"I'm talking about Seth Ryan. The actor," said Rudy.

"Me, too. We hung out at the Pizza Den last night."

Rudy laughed until someone else yelled, "It's true."

The voice came from behind me, and it seemed familiar, but not in a good way. Once I turned around I realized why. It was Seth's manager, Fiona. Or, more to the point, it was a very angry Fiona.

"This is Seth's *second* time disappearing," she told Rudy, pulling him aside, although not out of earshot, as if she didn't want me to be a *part* of the conversation, but she wanted me to know they were talking about me. "He first did so last night, and when I finally tracked him down, he was with her." She tilted her head toward me. "Which is highly suspicious, don't you think?"

Rudy looked from Fiona to me. "Is this true, Maggie?" he asked.

"Well, yes," I replied. "But the last time I saw Seth, Fiona was practically dragging him away."

"Which was in his best interest and which I have every right to do as his manager and legal guardian," she said to Rudy. "Part of my job is protecting Seth from the riffraff."

"The what?" I asked, butting in. "Are you actually calling me 'riffraff'? What does that even mean?"

"Let's all calm down," said Rudy. He turned to me. "Please, Maggie. Is there any shred of truth to what Fiona is saying?"

I gulped. "There is, but it's not like she says."

I explained what happened, how Seth approached me. Rudy listened carefully and took a lot of notes while I talked. "I know it sounds crazy, but I swear it's true." I tried to give him as much detail as possible. "And that's when Fiona came in and whisked him away. So as you can see, this has all been a gigantic misunderstanding."

"Uh-huh," said Rudy. "Got it."

"Good," I said. "I should probably get going."

"Not so fast," Rudy said as he placed his pen in his shirt pocket. "I think you'd better come with me."

"Where?" I asked.

"Down to the station."

Chapter 14

◆ ◆ ◆

I'd never been to a real police station before; it's not like it is on TV. I didn't see any hard-boiled criminals scream- ing about their innocence and struggling to break free as they were led away in handcuffs. Nor did I see any soft-boiled criminals, or any over-easy or sunny-side-up ones, either.

The room was a maze of desks with police officers scurrying between the rows like hamsters. None of them sported cheap-looking suits or funny mustaches. Not that there's any such thing as a non-funny mus- tache; I'm just saying, the entire scene was not at all what I'd pictured.

Of course, it's not like I actually got arrested or offi- cially accused of anything. I didn't even ride down to the precinct in a police car, which is lucky, I suppose. It's because I had Preston with me—a built-in excuse for not being able to go with Rudy at that very moment. I promised I'd go to the station later that day, and Rudy promised me if I didn't show up he'd find me. "Don't worry," he said. "We've still got your address on file from the dognapping bust."

Like that was supposed to reassure me!

As soon as I brought Preston home, I ran upstairs and called my mom and convinced her that this was real and not some elaborate prank. She told me to take the bus down to the precinct and to wait outside on the steps for her. "Do not walk through those doors alone—do you understand? I need to be there with you."

"Do most kidnapping suspects show up with their mothers?" I couldn't help but ask.

"Nope," my mom replied crisply. "But I'm not going to be there as your mother. I'm going to be there as your lawyer."

"Yikes!" I said.

"Yikes, exactly," she replied. "Now be sure to wear something nice. That means no jeans. And I'll see you there at six o'clock sharp. Remember—do not enter the building without me, and do not talk to anyone."

After I hung up, I changed into a skirt and tights and boots. Then I stared at myself in the mirror, trying to figure out if I looked guilty. I mean, obviously I'm innocent, but the whole being-summoned-to-police-headquarters-for-questioning-in-a-major-kidnapping-case thing made me feel like I'd done something wrong. And I hoped my nervousness didn't show. I was there to share information as a witness. This was what I reminded myself to quell my jitters once we finally sat down with Rudy and two other detectives at 6:05 that night.

Officers Flinti and Guererra were both short and roundish. Officer Guererra had a Spanish accent and a goatee. Officer Flinti was black and clean shaven.

After introductions, Rudy asked me to explain my encounter with Seth Ryan in my own words, using as much detail as possible.

"But I already did that," I said.

"I know, Maggie. But we need to hear it again," said Rudy.

I looked to my mom, who nodded for me to go ahead.

I took a deep breath and started talking. "I was at the Pizza Den last night, saving a table for my friends, when suddenly Seth Ryan was standing over me asking if he could ask me something. Which sounds redundant, I know, but that's exactly how it happened."

"He just picked you out of the crowd?" asked Officer Guerrera, looking like he didn't believe me.

"Yes," I said. "I mean, no. Not exactly. We'd talked on the movie set by his trailer two days before."

"So you *were* stalking him," said Officer Flinti, writing something down in his notebook.

"Objection," said my mother. "My client never stalked the victim. Please don't put words into her mouth or we're out of here."

I shot my mom a nervous glance. She smiled and winked and gestured for me to continue.

I took a deep breath and tried to re-create the scene as best I could. "No, I was just walking off the set and I passed by his trailer and I saw him waving. At first I figured he had to be talking to someone else, but no—it was me."

"We were told that right before you were thrown off the movie set you caused a public disturbance," Officer Guerrera said, checking his notes as if to verify this fact.

"Hardly!" I said. "All I did was try to leave. Jones Reynaldo was the one who freaked out. I wanted to stay, but I had to get to work—something I tried to tell him as politely as possible. But he wouldn't listen."

"So you have nothing against Seth Ryan?" Rudy asked.

"No, I love Seth Ryan," I said, then, realizing how that sounded, I tried to backtrack. "I mean, I like him. A lot. As in, I'm a fan, and based on our conversation, he seems like a nice guy. Not at all like I'd pictured him. Not that I didn't think he'd be nice. He's a total puppy dog."

Officer Flinti leaned a little closer. "Excuse me?"

"What?" I asked.

"Did you just call Seth Ryan a dog?" Officer Flinti asked.

"No, no. I mean, yes. Kind of, but not literally. What I mean is, he's sweet like a puppy dog. And a little lost."

"Not just lost," said Officer Flinti. "Missing, because he was kidnapped."

"I meant before he was kidnapped," I clarified.

My hands, which were resting on the table, began to tremble. My mom grabbed one. "Relax," she whispered.

"You say you're a big Seth Ryan fan," said Officer Flinti. "So why aren't you in his fan club?"

"How did you know about that?" I asked.

"We have our ways," Rudy said ominously.

"Well then, you also must know there are only two people in the Seth Ryan fan club," I replied, sitting up straighter. "Beatrix Williams and Sonya Singh."

They gave me blank stares.

I shifted in my seat and glanced at my mom. She smiled, encouraging me. I didn't know why I was nervous. I hadn't done anything wrong. "I like admiring Seth unofficially," I said finally.

"Like at the Pizza Den," said Officer Flinti.

"I already told you, he approached me. I was just sitting there, waiting for my pizza."

"What kind of pizza?" asked Rudy.

"Pepperoni with extra cheese," I fired back.

"And if we go to the Pizza Den and ask them about your order, they'll confirm it?" asked Officer Flinti.

"Well, I doubt the Pizza Den will remember. They were packed that night. And they're not exactly known for their great service. Plus, I was saving our table; my brother took care of the order."

"I see," said Rudy. "That's very interesting."

Officer Flinti grunted and the three of them exchanged a look.

This was weird. It was like they were playing a game. Trying to intimidate me or trick me into saying something incriminating when I had absolutely nothing to hide.

In this way, I did kind of feel like I was on some crime drama, which might've been cool, if not for one simple fact: someone had kidnapped Seth Ryan. It most definitely was not me. And the longer we sat there talking, the more time the real criminals had to get away.

Meanwhile, the officers just looked at me like they were waiting for something. I felt like I had to speak up. "No offense, but I think you're wasting your time. I've told you everything I know about Seth Ryan."

"So you say," said Officer Guerrera. "But I think we'll be the judge of that."

"Okay, this has gone too far," said my mother. "We

want to help, but obviously my daughter is innocent, and she has homework—you know, since she is in the seventh grade."

"We can't keep you here against your will," Rudy said, throwing up his hands. "And I think we're about done here, anyway. Thank you for your time, Maggie."

"Wait!" I said. "I've answered all of your questions, and now I have one question for you."

The detectives all looked at one another, surprised, I guess. Maybe I wasn't supposed to question them. Okay, I'm pretty sure I wasn't, but there was something I had to know. "What did the ransom note say?" I asked.

"We never claimed there was a ransom note," Officer Flinti said.

"You didn't tell me, but I overheard," I admitted.

No one looked at me. They seemed embarrassed, uncomfortable.

My mom put her hand on my shoulder. "Honey, we should go. That's not the kind of information they can share with civilians."

Just then Rudy coughed. "No, it's okay. Someone leaked it to the press, and it's going to be all over the media tomorrow morning anyway. So we can tell you." He flipped through his notes and then read the message. "It said, 'We have the boy. Don't bother looking. You'll never find him.'"

Chapter 15

• • •

My mother and I didn't speak for the entire six-block walk to the subway. Nor did we say anything as we headed down the dirty concrete steps, or through the squeaky turnstile, or onto the platform. We both seemed too upset, too worried about poor Seth. That note.

As our train rumbled into the station, I decided something. I'd already tracked down stolen dogs and found a giant fortune. I couldn't think of any reason why I couldn't rescue one missing movie star.

I'd launch my own investigation, find those kidnappers, and save Seth Ryan.

In fact, I knew just where to begin.

Chapter 16

• • •

Beatrix and Sonya were more than willing to help out, which was lucky for me. Not only did they love Seth Ryan, they also knew more about the guy than anyone I'd ever met. So first thing Saturday morning, I went straight to Sonya's house.

"Welcome to our first official emergency meeting of the Seth Ryan Fan Club," said Sonya as I joined them on her bedroom floor. She knocked a miniature gavel on the ground. "I feel like we should make up T-shirts or something."

"This is serious business," said Beatrix.

"I know. I'm totally serious." Sonya pushed her braids off her shoulders and pouted, insulted. "T-shirts don't mean 'not serious.' It's the opposite—they're to commemorate the moments leading up to our rescuing of Seth Ryan from some evildoer."

"You love saying 'evildoer,' don't you?" I asked, since I'd already heard her say it three times in the past hour.

"I do," Sonya said with a small shrug. "I can't help it."

Both she and Beatrix were already wearing matching "I ❤ Seth Ryan" shirts, but I didn't bother pointing this out. Instead I said, "Let's hope we track down Seth before any T-shirts would make it back from the printer."

Sonya frowned, thinking. "Then maybe we should pre-order victory shirts."

"My mom says I have to stop spending my allowance on Seth Ryan memorabilia," said Beatrix. "Or, as she calls it, 'Seth Ryan junk.' But we can figure that out later. Let's just get started. Everyone present, say 'aye.'"

"Aye," said Sonya.

"Aye," said Beatrix.

"Do you two go through this every week?" I asked, since it was just the three of us on Sonya's bedroom floor.

"Just say 'aye,'" Beatrix told me. "We're running out of time."

"Aye," I repeated.

Sonya looked around the room. "Should we wait for Lucy?"

"No, she called and said she had too much homework this weekend," said Beatrix.

"But we have all the same classes, practically, and there's actually not that much work," I said.

"We're not here to talk about Lucy," said Beatrix. "We're here to find Seth Ryan. Oh—and to welcome you to the official club."

Sonya turned to me with a serious expression. "Maggie, do you agree to uphold our founding principles and to accept all the rules and regulations of the Seth Ryan Fan Club?"

"Um, what are those rules?" I wondered.

"There's only one so far. You must really like Seth Ryan and promise not to do him or his image any harm," said Sonya.

"Oh, okay. I agree. Obviously, since I'm trying to help Seth here. So can we get on with things? I figure we should review anything and everything we know about the guy. That way we'll know where to look for clues, and we can also come up with a list of suspects."

"No problem." Sonya reached under her bed and dragged out the enormous and obviously titled *Seth Ryan Scrapbook*. Then she heaved it into the middle of our circle.

"So you went for the extra-big notebook?" I asked.

"Nope. This is just the first one," said Beatrix, pulling out another. Both notebooks were green—Seth's favorite color. "Let's start from the beginning." She opened the notebook to page one. "Seth was born on a cold wintry night in January. Same year as all of us! Sadly, his mother died soon after his first birthday. She got this rare and extremely aggressive form of cancer before he even learned to walk."

I shivered. "That's terrible. Poor guy!"

Beatrix and Sonya nodded, and then Beatrix cleared her throat and continued. "That meant his father took care of him, solo, in Buffalo, New York. That's upstate— almost in Canada."

I nodded. "Yeah. Seth told me he's from Buffalo."

Beatrix looked up from her notebook, exasperated. "Okay, we know you got to hang out with Seth Ryan last week, but you don't have to rub it in!"

"Sorry," I said. "I didn't mean to."

"Let's just skip to his first big break," said Sonya. "I doubt all this other stuff is relevant, and we don't know much about Seth's first year."

"Okay, you're right." Beatrix turned the page. "When Seth was little, his dad owned a used-car lot called Bill's of Buffalo."

"His dad's name is Bill," said Sonya.

"Thanks," I said. "I figured."

Beatrix went on. "He put Seth in a local car commercial when Seth was one and a half. In it, Seth was shown driving an old red pickup while singing the Bill's of Buffalo theme song and wearing a blue cowboy hat."

"Even back then, people noticed his smile. How it kind of lit up his whole face," Sonya said.

I bent over the notebook and looked at the baby pictures of Seth. It was true. "He already looked like a star. Even as a baby."

"He has the kind of face you can't forget, which is exactly what an advertising executive from New York City thought when he was in town for business and happened to turn on the TV in his hotel room," Sonya explained.

"It was serendipitous, really," said Beatrix. "This man was supposed to fly in and out of town on the same day, but then Buffalo got slammed with five feet of snow. No flights were getting out, and they even closed all the roads out of town. The guy got stuck in Buffalo for three whole days. He was flipping through the channels on the TV in his hotel room, looking for the local weather, when he became mesmerized by a singing, smiling boy."

"Do you guys know what Seth was singing?" I wondered.

"Do we?" asked Sonya. She and Beatrix smiled at each other and then jumped to their feet.

"We are Buffalo Bill's
Next to the old mill
Right off Route Ten

And we'll tell you again
We are Buffalo Bill's
Next to the old mill
Right off Route Ten
Don't mistake us for a hen
Come on in
Don't be shy
We've got cars, trucks, and smiles
All of which will run for miles!"

I laughed and clapped as they took their bows. "That was awesome. Have you guys been practicing?"

"No, we've just seen the commercial a bunch of times on YouTube. Want to check it out?" asked Sonya. She grabbed her laptop and found the commercial before I had time to agree, although I would have.

On the screen, a baby Seth sang his heart out like a pint-size pro. He had the same shaggy dark hair, big brown eyes, and magical smile.

"He's so cute," I said. "And he looks so much like himself. I mean, I guess that doesn't make a lot of sense, but—"

"But I know exactly what you mean," Sonya agreed. "He's, like, a natural-born star. Even as a baby."

"Exactly," I said, marveling at the clip. "It's wild."

"The advertising executive was in the middle of casting a national diaper commercial, and after he saw Seth in the car ad, he knew he'd be perfect," Beatrix explained. "So he called Buffalo Bill's and asked where he could find the kid. When Seth's dad answered, he thought it was a prank call. Because why would someone from the city be in Buffalo? And calling during a blizzard? That's why he laughed and hung up."

Sonya interrupted. "The guy called back, but Seth's dad still didn't believe him. So finally the guy borrowed some snowshoes and trudged all the way over to Bill and Seth's house to prove himself."

"He offered on the spot to fly Bill and Seth down to New York City for the shoot," said Beatrix. "And Bill figured, why not? He could use a change of scenery, and Seth always liked airplanes in theory. Why not give him a chance to ride on one in real life? He figured it would be a fluke, a one-time thing."

"But it was not a one-time thing," Sonya said. "The commercial went international and the company sold a record number of diapers."

"Seth Ryan became the most famous baby in the world. After the diaper campaign, his image was used to sell baby food, toy trains, Legos, swing sets, toy boats, and organic chicken strips."

Beatrix flipped through the scrapbook, showing me all of Seth's old ads. Each page showed him posing near a product and looking a little bit older. It was funny watching him grow up this way—kind of like his baby book was sponsored by tons of different companies.

"By the time he was four, he was the most photographed child in the world. According to what we've read, his career became difficult to manage, so Bill sold his used-car lot and began representing Seth full time, as his agent. And when that became too complicated, he hired Fiona to act as manager. She's the one who helped Seth make the jump from modeling to acting. Which meant moving to Hollywood."

"How old was he when he moved?" I asked.

"Eight. That's when he got his own show: *Wonderful Sam*. And that's when his acting career really took off," Sonya said.

I flipped through Beatrix and Sonya's scrapbook and glanced at the countless number of pictures of a smiling Seth Ryan.

"When he turned ten, he was a huge star," said Beatrix. "And Fiona and Bill started fighting over his career." She held up a second notebook. "This book covers the Fiona years: Seth from age nine to the present, when he went from being in movies to starring in movies, and then from starring in a movie a year to starring in two movies a year."

"By the time he turned eleven, he had his own

lunchbox, an action figure, a line of surfwear, a line of sportswear, sunglasses and sneakers, three official biographies, a coffee table book, and two albums," said Sonya. "She really did wonders for his career!"

"Something his dad resented," said Beatrix. "At least that's what some people say. Others even claim his dad mistreated him. Stole his money and exploited his image."

"Do you think that's true?" I wondered. I thought back to my encounter with Seth at the Pizza Den. How when his dad came up he acted so vague, clearly not wanting to talk about the guy. Was his dad that awful?

"Two years ago, Seth broke his arm snowboarding on a half-pipe for a movie about a hotel hit by an avalanche—*Snowed Inn*. According to some, Seth's dad pressured him to do his own stunts for the publicity," Sonya said. "And that's basically when Bill and Fiona both got lawyers and began fighting for custody of Seth."

"Can I see that?" I asked.

Sonya and Beatrix handed over the notebook. I read a bunch of articles about the battle between Seth's dad and his manager.

According to Bill, he wanted Seth to take a break from acting and go back to regular school.

According to Fiona, Bill was trying to steal money from his son and sabotage his entire career.

And according to Seth . . . Well, this seemed strange. I read three more articles and could not find any actual quotes or opinions from Seth.

"This is so weird," I said. "It looks like Seth never had anything to say about this."

"He must have," said Sonya. "It's his life." She read over my shoulder. "But you're right, there's nothing here. Funny how I never noticed that before."

"Maybe they couldn't print his statements because he's a minor," said Beatrix. "Anyway, in the end the lawyers decided that Seth would become an emancipated minor. That meant he could do whatever he wanted, and I guess he wanted to act, because he chose Fiona."

"It seems kind of strange, choosing your manager over your own father," said Sonya.

"Yeah," I agreed. "Especially when your manager has Fiona's toxic personality."

"But who knows what Seth's dad was really like? Maybe worse," Beatrix said. "Once his dad lost custody, Seth filed a restraining order against him. That means his dad isn't allowed to come within five hundred feet of him."

"He must be worse," said Sonya.

"Maybe." I closed the notebook and tried to make sense of it all. There was too much information. I didn't know where to begin. What I needed to do was simplify things. "Let's make a list of suspects," I said, pulling out my notebook.

"Good idea," said Beatrix. "Obviously we should put Seth's father on the list. And Fiona, too. You know, maybe one of them kidnapped him to get back at the other. It only makes sense, since they've been fighting over him for so long."

I wrote their names in my notebook and stared at them.

Doggie Deets

SUSPECTS
Seth's dad: Bill Ryan
Seth's manager: Fiona Stern

"Fiona is pretty uptight and overly protective," I said. "But as his manager, she gets a percentage of his salary. So I don't know if she would have a motive to kidnap him."

"Then it must be his dad," said Beatrix.

"Maybe," I said. "But what kind of dad kidnaps his own kid and leaves such a threatening note?"

"Good point. Hey, what about that lady, Jenna?" asked Beatrix. "The one who keeps fighting with Jones Reynaldo about filming on her street?"

"Oh, come on. She's friends with my parents," I said. "She probably drives a station wagon."

Sonya raised her eyebrows. "Station wagons have oversize trunks. Perfect for hiding kidnapping victims. Plus, she threatened to shut down the movie."

I couldn't deny any of this, but I still had my doubts.

"I'll talk to her," I said, adding Jenna Beasely to the list—just to make my friends happy. "And I can talk to Fiona, too, since we've already met a couple of times. Or I'll try to, anyway." I looked at my list. "So that's three suspects. Anyone else?"

"What about Brandon Wilson?" asked Beatrix.

"Who's that?" I asked.

"You know—that other actor we saw on the set of *Vanished*. He's got a small part, and check this out." Beatrix flipped through her scrapbook to an article about Brandon. "Apparently, he was supposed to get the lead in *Vanished,* but they gave it to Seth at the last minute."

I read the piece. Brandon Wilson was quoted as saying, "If it weren't for Seth Ryan, I'd be the biggest teen sensation . . ."

"That's pretty crazy," I said.

"We'll talk to Brandon," Sonya said. "We need to be at the set tomorrow, anyway."

"On a Sunday?" I asked. "With the star of the movie missing?"

Beatrix nodded. "Jones is insisting that the show must go on."

"Interesting," I said. I kind of wanted to add Jones Reynaldo to the list of suspects, just because he'd acted like a jerk. But I couldn't think of any motivation he'd have for kidnapping Seth. After all, it's not like he'd sabotage his own movie.

"Do you mind if I take this notebook home?" I asked.

"Go ahead," said Sonya. "But be careful with it. We've already lost Seth Ryan in the flesh; let's not lose all his pictures, too."

Since I passed by Lucy's house on my way back home anyway, I decided to knock on her door to find out why she hadn't been at Sonya's. I also figured she'd want to be filled in on the Seth Ryan search. Except no one answered.

This wasn't too big of a deal, I thought as I continued walking down the street.

Lucy could've been lots of places.

But I never would have guessed she'd be where I found her.

Chapter 17

• • •

"Um, hi?" I asked, walking into my living room, where Lucy and Finn were playing video games and giggling, so wrapped up in each other they didn't even notice.

"Lucy?" I tried again.

"Hey, Maggie," she said as she scrambled to her feet.

"What are you doing here?" I asked.

She flashed me a guilty smile. "I stopped by to see if you wanted to hang out. And you weren't here. So Finn invited me in. We were just playing *Hoops Away*."

"That's *Hoops Today*," said Finn.

"Right." Lucy giggled. "*Hoops Today*."

"We had plans to meet up at Sonya's this morning, remember? The Seth Ryan search."

"Oh, yeah." Lucy looked down at her blue Converse high-tops. She'd drawn a little brown owl on each of the rubber tips—owls she now stared at like they were a part of our conversation. "I kind of forgot."

"Beatrix told me you called her, specifically to say you couldn't make it."

"You need to call her Lulu now," Finn replied, as if that actually made sense.

"Huh?" I asked.

Finn and Lucy looked at each other without speaking, like they had their own secret language.

"Will someone please tell me what's going on?" I asked.

"I'm changing my name back to Lulu," Lucy said finally, with an easy shrug.

"What does that even mean?" I asked, now confused *and* a little alarmed.

"Lulu is what my parents called me when I was a baby, and it was only when I started kindergarten that I became Lucy," she explained. "It's because my teacher insisted that everyone use their given names. You know—the official ones from their birth certificates? And Lucy is my real name. Except I'd totally forgotten about that, so when she called roll on that first day, I didn't even know she was talking to me. And once I realized, I never said anything, because I guess I was just too shy. But I've always liked Lulu better. Plus, there are tons of Lucys in this neighborhood, and hardly any Lulus, so I'm going to be one of them."

"Lulu?" I asked, trying and failing to keep the question out of my voice. The name felt too strange on my tongue. It just didn't seem right. Of course, neither did discovering your best friend would rather hang out with your brother on a Saturday afternoon, even when you two obviously had plans. And not just any plans—major ones. I mean, what's up with that? "I don't know if I can get used to this."

"Well, you'll have to," said Finn, standing next to Lucy—I mean Lulu—so they were shoulder to shoulder, a united front.

"Don't you like it?" asked Lucy/Lulu.

Finn answered for me. "Of course she does. It's cute."

Lucy/Lulu beamed at my brother. "You really think it's cute?"

"I've never heard you use the word 'cute' in your entire life," I said to Finn.

Lucy/Lulu handed me the controls. "Want to finish my game? I've gotta go." And she was gone before I could answer her.

Once we were alone, I turned to Finn. "Why did she come over to see me, only to leave before we had a chance to hang out?" I asked.

Finn smirked and replied, "It's a mystery."

I had to agree, even though I sensed he was making fun of me. My brother is so weird. So is my best friend, for that matter. How many twelve-year-olds just up and change their name?

I didn't bother asking any more questions. Finn and I went back to playing *Hoops Today* in silence. He beat me three straight games in a row. No shocker there; I could hardly pay attention to the game.

The problem was, this one thought kept nagging at me: what if Lucy was changing more than her name?

• • •

Chapter 18

NEW EVIDENCE PROVES SETH RYAN WAS ABDUCTED BY ALIENS
SETH RYAN WAS LAST SEEN ON THE CROSSTOWN BUS
AT MIDNIGHT WITH NO SHOES
Superstar Seth Ryan Spotted in Mexico. . . .
In Pakistan . . . IN PERU **. . . in Paris . . .**
in a Pink Tutu

News of Seth Ryan's kidnapping spread fast. It was all anyone could talk about. Not just at school and in my neighborhood, but all over the world. Every newspaper, magazine, TV news channel, Twitter feed, and blog seemed to have a different take on his disappearance. Some were outlandish; some were insanely outlandish. People blamed the FBI, the CIA, the Russian Mafia, the Tea Party supporters, and China.

Paparazzi swarmed through our neighborhood.

Helicopters rumbled across the sky. Detectives canvassed the streets, questioning pretty much everyone within a ten-block radius of the set of *Vanished*.

Not only did no one find Seth, no one even knew where to look. Including myself.

But that wouldn't discourage me from trying.

I woke up early on Sunday and headed over to Second Street. Just like my friends had said, *Vanished* was still in production, but the entire set now had a different feel. People still filmed background scenes, changed the scenery, and built new snowmen and igloos as the old ones melted in the sun, but everyone did so quietly, more seriously. There was less hustle and bustle and less random chatter. From where I stood, on the corner and back a ways so I could observe without being caught staring, everyone seemed so serious—so obviously preoccupied with thoughts of Seth Ryan.

After saying hi to Beatrix, Sonya, Lucy, and Finn, who were sitting around waiting to be told where to stand and carefully avoiding Jones Reynaldo, who was yelling at someone on the other side of the block, I walked over to Jenna Beasely's house. I checked the address on the door against the one in my notebook: 555 Second Street. It matched. I took a deep breath and knocked.

The door swung open almost immediately, and I found myself standing in front of a cute blond teenage guy eating a granola bar. "Yeah?" he said, after swallowing.

"Does Jenna Beasely live here?" I asked.

Rather than answer me, he turned around and bellowed, "Mom! Someone's here for you." And then he walked away, leaving the door wide open.

Moments later, I heard Jenna's heels clicking on the wood floors, and then I saw Jenna herself. Blond hair pulled back in a ponytail, she was dressed in navy blue suit pants and an untucked, cream-colored dress shirt. "Can I help you?" she asked.

"I hope so. My name is Maggie Brooklyn Sinclair. I'm—"

"Elaine and Joe's daughter," Jenna finished.

"Yup, that's me." I smiled, relieved she remembered because questioning her as a complete and total stranger would have been weird. Or weirder, anyway. "Mind if I ask you some questions?"

"Not at all. Please come in." Jenna tilted her head and stared at me, curious and clearly surprised to see me. I didn't blame her.

"Cool. Thanks." I stepped inside.

As she led me into her living room, she asked, "Can I get you something to drink? Lemonade? Water? A soda?"

"No, thanks." I pulled out my notebook and pen,

feeling very Nancy Drew-ish. "And I won't take up too much of your time. I just have a few questions about Seth Ryan. Well, Jones Reynaldo, really. And the whole film shoot . . ." I felt flustered and not sure of what to ask first. I hadn't questioned that many people before, and it's harder than it sounds. Especially when one of those people is a friend of my parents. I didn't want to do anything embarrassing that might get back to them. Nor did I want to seem nosy or accusatory in any way. But at the same time, I needed information.

"Are you writing something about the kidnapping for your school paper?"

"Not exactly," I said, deciding to be straightforward. "I'm in the middle of an investigation. I'm hoping to find Seth Ryan."

"You and everyone else," Jenna replied. "If you want to talk about Seth Ryan, that's fine. We can, but I don't think I can help you. The police have already questioned me—although I have no idea why."

"Maybe because you threatened to shut down the movie in front of about fifty witnesses?" I asked, as delicately as I could.

"I threatened to shut down the movie by calling the police. I'd certainly never break the law. Or harm anyone—especially an innocent child. And from a purely selfish point of view, I'd much rather have a movie filmed on my street than have the place crawling with police and detectives and paparazzi. It's true that I don't want to live in the middle of a movie set. Well, I don't want to live in the middle of a crime scene, either, or have the police search my house and bring me downtown so they can run my fingerprints and then later question everyone in my family and everyone at my office."

"Rudy did that?" I asked.

Jenna tilted her head and narrowed her eyes at me. "You're on a first-name basis with Officer Green?"

"I am." I gave her a quick smile. "Long story."

"Well, it's been quite the ordeal," said Jenna, crossing her legs and smoothing out her suit pants. "And all because I had a perfectly legitimate grievance with one perfectly childish director."

"Sorry," I said. "That does sound pretty awful."

"It *has* been, but it's not your fault, and I'm sorry—I don't mean to take out my frustrations on you. I'm a reasonable person. Truly, I am. Jones just brings out the worst in me. I wouldn't even mind one movie shoot on my street, but this is the fourth time they've shut down Second Street this month."

"Why do they always film here?" I asked. "No offense; it's a nice street and everything. But there are lots of nice streets in the neighborhood."

"I know. The reason all of these productions come

here is my neighbors, the Franklins. They rent their house out to production companies all the time; it's a great deal for them. They get paid, and then they leave town. It's everyone else around them who suffers. Last summer, for example, during the Tom Cruise shoot, one of the catering trucks backed into my scooter. Flattened it, actually. And, sure, they paid to replace it, but it took months."

"That does sound annoying," I said.

"And during a shoot last spring, they brought in a weather machine and it rained into my backyard and overwatered my tulips. I spent an entire weekend planting bulbs, for nothing. They never blossomed."

"Wow."

I scribbled notes as fast as I could, but it wasn't easy keeping up with Jenna. She was worked up and talking fast.

"And don't even get me started on Jones Reynaldo. You would not believe the ego on this guy. Did you know that he wanted to film one small scene in Prospect Park and tried to get a permit to shut it down in its entirety?"

I shook my head. "I didn't know that."

"Well, did you realize that the park is three miles long and almost a mile wide? Meanwhile, he only wanted to shoot by the Nethermead. You know, that field close to the Ninth Street entrance?"

"So why did he need the whole park?" I wondered.

Jenna laughed. "He claimed there are too many dogs, which is distracting for him because he's highly allergic. And also, his movie *Vanished* takes place in a futuristic society where there are none, and sound carries in the park. He claimed he needed the entire area, and he's perfectly willing—if not eager—to inconvenience the thousands of people who use the park every single day—people who live and pay taxes in Brooklyn—for his precious movie."

"And this was rejected, I take it?"

"Yes, it was rejected. I'm on the board of the Parks Department, and I wasn't going to let that type of thing happen."

"You're on the board of the Parks Department?" I asked, suddenly thinking of Mister Fru Fru and all the other victims I'd been hearing about. "Have you heard about the recent dog-eggings in the park?"

"I have." Jenna frowned. "It's really terrible. I mean, if this is someone's idea of a prank, they've got problems."

"What makes you think it's a prank?" I asked, leaning a little closer.

Jenna shrugged. "I don't know—I just can't think of any other feasible explanation. Anyway, they seemed to have lost interest. Have you noticed that there have been no new eggings since Seth disappeared?"

"Yeah, I checked the blogs this morning and didn't see any new posts. I figured whoever is responsible is afraid of getting caught. You know, because of all the police around town."

Jenna nodded. "That makes sense. Anyway, I have a feeling Jones did some research and found out about my position, because he's been making things extra difficult on me ever since."

"How so?" I asked.

"Well, he put Seth Ryan's trailer right in front of my house, blocking all my light and the entire view of the street. Notice that all the other trailers are set back away from the sidewalk—but Seth's is practically on my front stoop."

"I figured that was a security measure," I said.

"Nope," Jenna said. "It's just to bug me."

I stood up and looked out Jenna's window. She had a direct view of Seth's trailer. "It looks like you'd be able to see him from here."

"I could," said Jenna. "Not that I spent too much time watching him."

"Did you notice anything strange? Anyone going in or out of his trailer?" I asked.

"Well, there was some sort of disturbance on Wednesday. Apparently, a stalker had to be apprehended by his security guard. I was working at the time, but my son, Jonas, was home . . ."

I didn't bother clearing up that mistake. Instead, I closed my notebook and stood up. "Well, I guess I'm out of questions. Thanks so much for your time, Jenna. I appreciate it."

"Of course, Maggie. I'm impressed that you're conducting this investigation; I wish you all the luck in the world. I hope Seth is okay. Truly, I do. Please let me know if I can help you in any other way."

"I will," I said.

"And say hello to your parents. We should all go out to brunch sometime."

Chapter 19

✦ ✦ ✦

After my last run-in with Fiona, I doubted she'd be willing to speak with me, but when I called her at her hotel
and asked if we could talk about Seth, she surprised
me. "Sure. Let's meet at Root Hill at three o'clock today."

She seemed to take my silence at the other end of
the line for confusion—and rightfully so.

"Do you know the place?" she asked moments later.

"Um, I don't, but I'll find it," I replied, still stunned.
And a few hours later, I realized that locating the café
turned out to be simple compared to spotting Fiona in
the crowd. She looked terrible, like she hadn't slept in
days. Her eyes were ringed with red and her hair was
not just poofy, but a poofy mess. At first glance I didn't
recognize her. She clutched her coffee with both hands,
as if guarding it from someone who wanted to steal it.
And when she raised it to her lips, her fingers trembled.

I didn't like how Fiona had treated me, or how she treated Seth, or how she walked around like she was the boss of everything and everyone. She was like a classic villain in a movie, but we needed to work together. After all, we both had the same goal—rescuing Seth. That was more important than anything else.

"How are you doing?" I asked, just to be polite, even though I could pretty much tell. All the anger had drained out of her, leaving her looking weary, worried, and lonely.

"Terrible," she said, blinking back tears.

Despite how she'd talked to me last week, I felt bad for her. "Does Rudy have any new leads?" Half of me had hoped that by the time we met, Seth would be rescued, or at least someone would know where to look for him, but clearly that hadn't happened.

Fiona shook her head slowly. "No one has a clue," she said, her voice cracking as she struggled to hold back her emotions.

"I'm sorry," I said sincerely. "It's hard for me to imagine he's still missing, and I hardly know him. It's got to be so much worse for you."

"It's horrifying," Fiona said as she took another sip of coffee. "I never had children of my own. I didn't need to, because I had Seth. I've poured my heart and soul into that boy's career. Loved him like my own son.

I just can't believe he's gone, that someone would kid-nap him. And why? Not knowing is just torture."

I leaned in closer, studying her face. "Do you have any idea who could've done this?"

"None," Fiona cried. "Which means it could be anyone. A crazed fan, an embittered colleague, a Swed-ish diplomat . . ."

"A Swedish diplomat?" I asked, writing this down. "Why do you think—"

"I don't," said Fiona. "But no one ever suspects Swed-ish diplomats of anything, and I'm just saying, the police have absolutely nothing to go on. They've questioned everyone, and they don't seem to know where to turn next. It would be different if the kidnapper asked for ran-som money. That's something the police have experi-ence with; but the radio silence? It's eerie." She shivered, which made me shiver, too.

"What about Seth's father?" I asked, watching her closely.

Fiona looked up from her coffee, surprised. "Why do you bring up Bill?" she asked.

"I read about the custody battle with Bill and the restraining order Seth put out against him."

She stared at me like she was trying to figure some-thing out. It made me squirm even though I didn't have anything to hide. "You've done your research."

"Yes. Of course." I tucked my hair behind my ears. "And I've read a bunch of conflicting accounts. So can you please tell me your side of the story?"

"Okay." Fiona took a deep breath and fluffed her hair with her fingers. "It's simple. Bill's a nice guy, but he's a used-car salesman. That's the business he knows, and that's the business he should stick with. I'm a talent manager, and I have been for my whole life. We had different opinions about what would be best for Seth and for Seth's career. We couldn't agree about it. We took it to court. I won and he left. And Seth's better off. Trust me." She took another sip of coffee, setting it down with a clatter. Her hands trembled, which made me curious. Fiona seemed not merely grief-stricken, but also nervous. I wondered why.

"But why the restraining order?" I asked.

"I can't talk about that," said Fiona.

I leaned closer to her and lowered my voice. "Do you think Bill could have kidnapped Seth? Like, as revenge? Or in some twisted way, did he want his son back and maybe he felt like this was the only way he could accomplish it?"

"I don't know," said Fiona. "I certainly wouldn't put it past him. And that's exactly what I told the police. But detectives have already questioned Bill. If he's hiding Seth, he's doing an excellent job."

"Huh," I said, thinking about it.

Fiona looked at me, sizing me up. "You seem like a smart girl, but you can't expect to do what hundreds of professionals—with more resources and more experience—have been unable to do."

"I have to try, though."

"That's admirable," said Fiona. "And I'm sure it would mean a lot to Seth. I'm sorry if I spoke to you harshly back there at that Pizza Cave."

"Pizza Den," I said.

"Right. Maybe I got too worked up. You just never know with people. Someone was crazy enough to kidnap Seth. My—" She didn't finish her sentence. She seemed too upset to speak.

Suddenly, tears streamed down her face. I could tell she was the type of person who didn't often break down in public. That's probably why she rushed into the bathroom, locking the door behind her.

I sat there thinking, worried that Seth was in danger, frustrated at what seemed like such a hopeless situation.

When Fiona didn't return after a few minutes, I went to the door and heard muffled sobs over the rush of water. She must've turned on the sink to cover the anguished sounds, but it didn't work. I heard everything.

I knocked softly. "Are you okay, Fiona?"

"Fine," she sniffed through the door. "I mean, I'll be fine—eventually. Please just go. I'm sorry I can't help you. I just hope someone finds Seth before it's too late."

"I'll let you know if I hear anything," I promised.

Back at our table, I grabbed my backpack, and accidentally tripped over Fiona's bag. It was one of those fancy purses—shiny and oversize, and when it tipped over, half the contents spilled out.

I crouched down to pick them up and put her makeup and wallet and keys back in the bag. That's when I noticed the letter. I went to put it away, too, with the rest of her junk, but stopped once I noticed to whom it was addressed. Seth Ryan. And the return address? Bill Ryan, in Buffalo, New York.

I stood slowly as I stared at the letter. Something was written in the corner, faint pencil tracings I had to squint to read properly. The number sixty-seven. What did it mean?

I glanced at the closed bathroom door.

Fiona had just gone out of her way to tell me that Bill refused to speak to Seth. Does someone who refuses to speak to his son send a letter? A letter, I realized—glancing at the postmark—that was sent days before he disappeared?

I don't think so.

I quickly put the letter in my backpack, then righted Fiona's purse and headed out the door.

As I rushed home, my mind buzzed with a familiar feeling. Somehow I knew that I was on the brink of a major discovery.

No, I still didn't know where Seth was, and Fiona didn't, either.

She hadn't kidnapped him—that much seemed obvious.

But so was this: she sure was guilty of something.

Chapter 20

· · ·

When I got home, I sat down at my desk with the letter in front of me. My first instinct was to tear it open and read it to search for clues that could lead me to Seth.

I ran my fingers along the edge of the seal, then placed my pointer finger under the corner, but I couldn't go any further due to one simple fact: the letter was addressed to Seth. That meant the contents were private. This wasn't for my eyes, and I had to respect that.

Once I found Seth, I'd give it to him. And find him I would.

Since I didn't have any more actual leads, I decided to do some research online. I read more about the court case, and found that while Fiona hadn't bluffed, she'd only told me one side of the story.

While she'd claimed that Bill didn't know how to manage Seth's career, Bill had accused Fiona of working Seth too hard.

They also had differing accounts of how Seth broke his arm snowboarding. Bill claimed that Fiona pressured Seth into doing his own stunts. Fiona claimed it was Bill who forced him into it. I looked for Seth's account, but couldn't find it anywhere. The entire battle seemed to take place around him, as if Seth never had his own opinion—or, at least, none that got recorded.

Next I checked out the local newspaper in Buffalo. It seemed like the only place I hadn't looked.

Right away I saw an advertisement for Bill's of Buffalo. It looked like Seth's dad had started up his old business again.

SUVs were on sale. Prices like you've never seen before.

I did a Google search on Bill's of Buffalo and Bill Ryan.

And that's when a random link at the bottom of the page caught my eye. I clicked on it, and it led me to the local birth announcements. "Congratulations, Bill Ryan, on the birth of twin boys!" It was dated five weeks ago. Bill and someone I presumed to be his wife were standing in a parking lot with two blue bundles and gigantic smiles.

Bill Ryan was Seth's dad. And now, apparently, he was also dad to two new boys. That means Seth had two half brothers!

Of course, Seth had been estranged from his father

a long time. I wondered if he'd ever get to meet them. I wondered if he even knew they existed.

One glance at Bill's picture told me he did not kidnap his oldest son. His eyes were squinty from smiling so much, and I could see the joy on his face. Exhaustion, too. Even if he *were* the kind of guy who'd kidnap his own son, he certainly wouldn't be able to do it in the weeks following the birth of twins, I didn't think. He'd be too busy. So I crossed him off my list.

Still, I wondered what he'd written to Seth. Was Bill angry with Seth? Did he miss him? Was he sorry? Worried? Still confused? Did he simply write to give him the news? What did the number in the corner mean? Was it some sort of secret code? Would Seth know?

And why did Fiona hold on to the letter? I thought about her hands trembling when I asked her about Bill, and I realized she wasn't simply worried—she was terrified. But why?

Chapter 21

. . .

Charlotte was waiting for me at my locker when I got to school on Monday. "How's the investigation going?" she asked, instead of saying hello. That was her thing, I now knew. No "hi" or "bye" or "how are you?" or any other pretense. She was completely direct: *this is why I'm talking to you, and this is what I want.* Once I got used to it, I found her honesty refreshing.

"Oh, hey, Charlotte. Not great," I told her, deciding to be perfectly honest about my completely imperfect investigation. "I've found plenty of other victims. Six or seven dogs last week, all attacked at around the same spot; but no one I've talked to has seen the egger's face. Meanwhile, I've staked out the park on three different occasions, but I've never witnessed an attack, and I'm not sure of where to look next. Of course, there haven't been any new reports all weekend. And I've been a bit distracted these days."

"I'm sure," said Charlotte. "You're probably too worried about your boyfriend."

"My boyfriend?" I asked.

"It's okay." She leaned in close and lowered her voice. "You can tell me the truth."

Truth was, Milo would hardly speak to me these days. He's the closest thing I've ever had to a boyfriend, and he's currently further from being my boyfriend than he's ever been. Even before we'd ever spoken, I could imagine some future time when we would hang out and get to know each other and be friends before one thing would lead to another and we'd be a couple. But now? Not a chance. Which isn't anything I felt like sharing with Charlotte.

Nor could I understand why she would care.

Or how she would know.

In response to my blank stare, she pulled a copy of the *New York Post* out of her messenger bag and opened it to Page Six. There in the middle of the gossip section was a gigantic close-up of Seth Ryan and me.

"That is you, correct?" Charlotte asked.

"Um, yeah," I replied, taking the paper so I could get a closer look.

The picture was from when we shared a table at the Pizza Den. I mean, obviously, since that's the only time I'd been within five feet of him (without getting assaulted by his security guard, I mean).

It was certainly the only time we'd actually shared a real conversation. It's funny that it was documented.

On the other hand, I'd seen pictures of Seth riding a bike, eating apples, and tying his shoes. Pretty much his whole entire life was captured on film and then published for the entire world to see; why not this random encounter?

Of course, once I read the headline, I realized the *New York Post* thought our encounter was anything but random: *Seth and His New Mystery Girlfriend Share a Slice.*

The picture was taken from over my shoulder. Seth's entire face was visible, but only the back of my head. From that angle, it looked as if Seth was hunched over the table, staring into my eyes intensely. If it were anyone else but me in the shot, I'd probably assume Seth was on a date, too.

It all struck me as odd, because I didn't remember seeing any photographers or hearing any camera clicks. That someone had done this in secret—it was kind of creepy. And at the same time, almost cool. I'd made the news. Or at least "Mystery Girlfriend" had. People thought that Seth and I were an item. How hilarious! How bizarre! How exciting!

"I can't believe this," I said.

Charlotte took her newspaper back. "So, what's he really like?" she asked. "And how did you guys meet? How long have you been together? Have you been to

Hollywood? Does his house really have an arcade with a bowling alley and a Whac-a-Mole made out of gold?"

I didn't know what to say, so I remained silent. It wasn't just shock—it was also wonder. I'd never heard about Seth's gold Whac-a-Mole table. I wondered if it was true, and where he'd even get something like that.

"I'm sorry," said Charlotte. "I'm being insensitive. It stinks about your boyfriend. It must be agonizing for you. I hope he's okay."

"Yeah, me, too," I replied. "But Seth isn't my boyfriend. I hardly know him."

Charlotte smiled. "Let me guess. You can't let anyone know because you may be in danger, too, right? Whoever's got Seth might want to kidnap you next. I get it."

That thought had never occurred to me before. Maybe Charlotte had a point. I looked over my shoulder, wondering if maybe I should be more careful. No, wait a second. This was crazy. "Really, he's not my boyfriend."

"Right," said Charlotte, clearly not buying this. "I just hope you can still track down Mister Fru Fru's egger. I understand that you have a lot on your mind. Boyfriend missing, possibly kidnapped—it's rough. But Seth isn't the only one who needs you now. Anyway, he's got a gazillion people searching for him. But think about all the dogs in Prospect Park. All they have is you."

"Honestly, we've never even been on a date."

Charlotte smiled. "There's photographic evidence to prove it, but fine, stick with that story."

Before I could explain, she turned around and left.

No good-bye, of course.

On my way to homeroom, eight random people I didn't even know said hello to me. And before I got to class, a sixth grader named Tracy with short dark hair, glasses, and freckles cornered me and asked for my autograph.

"Are you kidding?" I asked. "I'm not famous."

"But your boyfriend is."

"He's not my boyfriend," I insisted.

She nodded. "I heard you had to say that, but don't worry. I won't tell."

I wanted to explain, but at the same time, it was so much easier to sign her notebook and go to class. At least that's what I thought before four of Tracy's friends saw me and insisted on autographs as well.

By lunchtime, my hand ached from signing so much. And my head ached from trying to figure out who kidnapped Seth and who the egger could possibly be. I couldn't wait to see my friends and have some normalcy.

But when I showed up at my regular table, Beatrix and Sonya were both wearing Sherlock Holmes–style detective hats. Sonya carried a magnifying glass in her shirt pocket and Beatrix chewed on a fake pipe.

"Can you believe these two?" asked Lucy, who was already halfway done with her spaghetti.

"I take it you guys spoke to Brandon?" I said.

"Oh, yeah. We cornered him last night after we were done with our scenes. It was awesome," said Sonya.

"He's totally guilty," said Beatrix. "It was all over his face. I mean, not literally. But I could tell."

Sonya shook her head. "Don't listen to her, Maggie. He's completely innocent. I'm sure of it."

"No, he's just acting that way so we don't suspect him," Beatrix insisted.

"How about you tell me what happened," I said.

"Good idea." Beatrix took her pipe out of her mouth. "We'll let the facts speak for themselves."

"Where did you get that thing, anyway?" I asked.

"My grandpa used to smoke it," said Beatrix. "I found it in a box with his old dentures."

"Ew!" the rest of us yelled.

"Well, I washed it first, obviously," said Beatrix.

"Let me start," said Sonya, consulting her notes. "We launched our investigation at seventeen hundred hours. That's five o'clock in the evening, military time."

"Thanks," I said.

"We approached the subject—that's Brandon—at Craft Services." She paused to look at me. " 'Craft services' is what they call the catered food at any movie or TV set. They have to feed people because of union regulations. Anyway, Brandon had just taken a medium-size bite of a turkey and cheese sandwich."

"Swiss cheese," said Beatrix. "And it had mustard on it, too. Which I know because some of it fell out of his sandwich and landed on his shirt by his collar."

"I see," I said. "And that relates to Seth's disappearance how?"

"In no way, shape, or form," said Sonya. "We just wanted to let you know that we were paying attention." She held up her notebook, the page filled with her careful handwriting. "And we've taken lots of notes."

"So what did Brandon say?"

"It was awesome. Beatrix went undercover. Meaning she pretended like she was a huge fan of his work."

Beatrix nodded excitedly. "And Sonya pretended to be British."

"Wait, what?" I asked.

"I pretended to be British," said Sonya, switching to an exaggerated British accent. "It was easy because my cousins from London were just visiting. So everything was spot-on, as they say."

"But how will pretending to be British help us track down Seth?" I wondered, baffled.

"Isn't it obvious?" asked Sonya. "All the great detectives are British. Sherlock Holmes. Agatha Christie's Miss Marple. Sherlock—wait, I already said him, right?"

Beatrix nodded. Sonya turned back to me. "It just felt right that way."

"Okay, fine. So what happened?"

"I swooned and asked for his autograph," Beatrix said. "And I told him how much I'd always wanted to meet him. He was thrilled, and went back into his dressing room to get me a headshot so he could sign that instead of the paper I offered him."

"He gave me a signed one, too," said Sonya. "Even though I didn't ask for it."

"It's true," said Beatrix. "And he thanked us both and said that usually people don't even recognize him. Especially when he's working with Seth. And I said, 'That must be annoying,' and he said, 'You have no idea' . . ."

"And then what?" I asked.

"What do you mean?" asked Beatrix.

"Um, what happened next?"

"I said 'Thank you' and he said 'See you later.' And he headed back to his trailer."

"Didn't you ask him about Seth's disappearance?" I asked.

"We didn't want to seem obvious," said Beatrix. "I figured we'd catch him by surprise."

"That's why we did surveillance," said Sonya. "That means we camped out across the street and watched his trailer for suspicious activity."

"Thanks," I said. "I know."

"Right. I'm forgetting you've been a detective for weeks now. It's still kind of new to us, but we're learning," said Sonya. "And check out my new binoculars. Pretty cool, huh?"

They were small and gray and lightweight. "These are nice." I raised them to my line of vision and aimed them at Milo, who sat on the other side of the cafeteria. He ate a burrito while bent over a book, alone. Not in an I-have-no-friends way; usually he ate with Finn's crowd. More like an I'm-too-busy-today-and-I'm-cool-enough-to-do-that way.

I wondered if he'd heard the rumor about Seth and me. Everyone at school seemed to think we were a couple. But Milo was there when I met him. He knew the truth. So why was he still acting so distant? In science this morning I asked him if he had a hard time with the homework, and he shrugged and said, "Not really," without even turning around.

"Maggie?" asked Sonya.

"Sorry." I returned the binoculars. "These are great. Very powerful. So, um, what did you see?"

"Nothing," said Sonya. "We watched his trailer for over an hour. He never came out. And then we had to go home and do our homework."

"You know our report on Cindy Singer is due tomorrow," Beatrix said.

"It's not due until Tuesday," I said.

"Right—and today is Monday," Sonya replied.

I cringed. "Yikes, I haven't even started."

"Then it's a good thing we solved the mystery," said Beatrix.

"We did?" I asked. "I think we're kind of missing some evidence."

"We don't need any more evidence," said Beatrix. "I told you—Brandon is obviously jealous of Seth's career and he's tired of always playing the sidekick and the best friend and the other, unnamed guy. It's been driving him insane. I just know it."

"Okay, that may be true, but it doesn't mean he'd kidnap him," I said.

"It doesn't mean he didn't," Beatrix replied.

"I guess you have a point. But how do we know the mail carrier isn't guilty? Maybe *she's* jealous of Seth's career, too."

Sonya nodded and added "mail carrier" to her notes, followed by three gigantic question marks.

"I don't really think the . . . never mind. Look, even if Brandon *is* guilty, we're still not done. We still need to figure out where Seth is. And, you know—rescue him."

"This is hard," said Beatrix.

I turned to Sonya. "Can you tell me why you think Brandon is innocent?"

"Sure. It's because he's sweet and he dresses really

cute. His shirt had a collar and it was tucked into his jeans and he wore a nice belt," she replied.

"I don't get it," I said.

"Think about it." Sonya tapped her forehead with one finger.

I looked at Beatrix, who held her head in her hands in frustration.

I turned to Lucy, I mean Lulu, to get her opinion, but was surprised to find that she wasn't sitting next to me anymore.

"Where's Lulu?" I asked.

"Who?" asked Sonya. "Oh—she's over there." Sonya pointed to the next table, where Lulu sat with Finn and his best friends, Red and Otto.

They were all laughing about something. No, scratch that. Lulu wasn't merely laughing—she was hysterical. I'm talking red-faced and shoulders shaking.

It's not like Lulu has to sit with me at lunch every day. But she *has* been sitting with me every day—up until ten minutes ago. So what was up?

"I wonder what she thinks about Brandon," I said.

"She's been pretty distracted lately," said Beatrix. "I don't think she's given it much thought."

"We tried to get her to question Brandon with us, but she was too busy," Sonya said. "It's like she doesn't even care about Seth Ryan."

Sonya was right, but that wasn't my biggest concern. Lucy acted like she didn't even care about me.

But before I could figure out what was going on with my current best friend, my ex–best friend showed up.

Her name is Ivy Jeffries, and usually she doesn't acknowledge me in public. Or in private. It's like she fears "unpopularity" is contagious. Except she must've taken antibiotics over the weekend, because now she stood over me with this huge smile on her face. "Hey, Maggie. Is it true?" she asked, sitting down next to me like we were still best buds.

"Is what true?"

She lowered her voice and leaned in close. "You know—the whole you-and-Seth-Ryan-being-a-couple thing."

I looked at Beatrix and Sonya, expecting them to blow my cover, but they stayed silent, watching us like we were the stars in some exciting new Web series— *Best Friends/Worst Enemies: Drama in the Lunchroom.*

Ivy waited, but I didn't know what to say to her. Obviously she was only here because she thought I was dating the most famous movie star in the world.

And I could've told her it was a big misunderstanding.

But at the same time, I didn't have to.

I grinned at her with the same sort of condescending grin she gave me all the time. Like when she'd first decided she didn't want to be friends with me but hadn't bothered telling me about it. Not even after I sat down with her and her new, better friends at lunch that first day of sixth grade. Or the day after that. Or the day after that. It took almost an entire week of me sitting with them—wondering why they were ignoring me—to figure it out. She'd moved on and didn't even have the decency to tell me about it. Not that I'm bitter. (Anymore.)

"I can't really talk about my relationship with Seth Ryan to the general public," I told her.

Her eyes got wide. "But I can keep a secret. You know—just between friends . . ."

"It's just too complicated," I said with an exaggerated shrug as I packed up my lunch. "You understand, Ivy. Right?"

Chapter 22

• • •

All the books on Cindy Singer were checked out of both the school and local libraries, so I'm lucky I still had the biography my mom tried to push on me last month. Especially considering my report on Cindy Singer was due in eighteen hours.

That night I cracked open the book and took notes as I read about Cindy's life and work.

Born in Hampstead, suburb of London
Studied at Goldsmiths—an art school in London
Nominated for Turner Prize—some big modern art award
Has a sculpture on display at the Tate, which is a famous gallery in London

According to the book, Cindy's artwork all revolved around a number of themes—one of those themes literally being the number three.

Her first real show consisted of gigantic threes con-
structed out of different materials: glass blown into the
shape of a three and filled with sand in three colors, a
three made out of three pieces of rope woven together,
and a neon three. Also, three statues of the number
one, tied together with three pieces of yellow string—
because yellow is the third color on the color spectrum.

The book also had a few pictures of the Hansel and
Gretel house exhibit Lulu had mentioned. One thing
she didn't tell us, though, was that the house was con-
structed with only three sides.

Despite the ants having eaten part of Cindy's sculpture, this piece seemed to launch her into a major fairy-
tale kick. After the Hansel and Gretel house, she created
a giant installation piece based on princesses, with
three poison apples, three glass slippers, and only six
of the seven dwarves: Happy, Sleepy, Doc, Dopey,
Sneezy, and Grumpy. Not three, but certainly divisible
by three.

She also had a show where she took pictures
of people dressed up as the three main characters of
"Little Red Riding Hood"—the girl, the grandmother,
and the wolf.

Once I read about an installation based on "Goldilocks and the Three Bears," I figured I had enough material to write my report, so I opened my laptop and started
a new document.

But as I tried to connect Cindy's current instal-lation—the two tree houses—to her earlier work, I found that something didn't make sense. Everything about Cindy Singer's art told me there should be a third tree house somewhere in the park. And also some kind of connection to a fairy tale.

When our teacher asked if there was a third tree house last week, Cindy had said no. But now that I knew more about her, something seemed fishy.

Cindy was clearly a very successful and well-established artist, used to working on her own terms. So why wouldn't she create three tree houses? And what did they have to do with fairy tales? Unless she was changing direction and the monk parakeets in Prospect Park were her new inspiration. Somehow I doubted it.

I closed my eyes and conjured up the houses in my mind. One was made of bricks and one was made of sticks. They were cool in their own right, but I couldn't help but feel like they also seemed incomplete.

Also, what type of fairy tale involved tree houses? Or even three houses? The answer was in some back corner of my brain that I couldn't quite access.

I scanned my bookshelf and then Finn's, searching for our old book of fairy tales. And then I remembered we sold it at our last stoop sale. So I grabbed my jacket and headed to the Community Bookstore, which is just around the corner. It's a musty old store with a stained red rug, a piano that no one's allowed to use, and a cat that likes to scratch children if they get too close.

They also have a decent kids' books section, which was all I really needed. I grabbed the first anthology of fairy tales I saw and sat down on one of their low chairs. I flipped to the table of contents and scanned the titles. "Goldilocks and the Three Bears," "Cinderella," "Sleeping Beauty," "Little Red Riding Hood," "The Ugly Duckling," "The Frog Prince," and "The Three Little Pigs."

And "The Three Little Pigs." That's it, exactly. I mean, obviously I knew the story—I'd heard it a gazillion and three times, but not lately. As I read, I realized I was on to something.

Each of the three pigs wanted to build a house of his own. The first pig made a house out of straw. The second pig made a house out of sticks. And the third pig made a house out of bricks.

I thought back to our morning in the park and pictured the house made out of bricks and the house made out of sticks.

And suddenly something clicked in my brain. Cindy *did* construct three tree houses. We'd seen the one made of sticks and the one made of bricks—and somewhere in the park was a third tree house. A secret tree house made out of straw.

But that's not all. I put the book away and raced home. Once in my room, I flipped through my Doggie Deets notebook, back to my early investigation of the dog-egger.

"The laughter came from above," said Cassie.

"It's like it came from nowhere," said Jane.

"I saw a guy in a black T-shirt appear from nowhere. It was like he was magical," said Milton with the mohawk.

It made total sense that the house was built on Ninth Street. The house of sticks was at Grand Army Plaza; the house of bricks at Third Street. Continue south to the next park entrance, and you have Ninth Street. Obviously Cindy had built a third, straw house near Ninth Street.

I still didn't know who the egger was. But something told me I'd just found his or her hiding spot. I put on my jacket and headed for the front door, and that's when I ran into my mom, who was just coming home from work.

"Where are you going?" she asked as she set her briefcase down by the coatrack.

"Um, Lucy's," I said.

"Doesn't she go by Lulu now?" asked my mom.

"Yeah—Lulu. I'm still getting used to it. But I really have to go."

"Isn't it a little late for a school night?" asked Mom.

"I won't be gone long."

I was halfway out the door when she said, "Before you go, can you give me your report on Cindy Singer? I think I'd like to read it while you're gone."

I froze and turned around. "I'm not quite done with it yet, but—"

"Maggie, it's six o'clock on a school night and your report is due tomorrow. You're not leaving this house."

I couldn't really argue with her logic—and I couldn't exactly tell her I needed to go to the park to find a straw house when it was already pretty dark out. Trudging back inside, I told her, "Okay. I'll finish that report now."

"Thank you," she replied.

Back in my room, I turned on my laptop and opened up my report.

I wrote about Cindy's life and work and her obsession with fairy tales and the number three. I wrote about the brick and stick houses being inspired by "The Three Little Pigs." And I wrote that there must be a third house somewhere in the park—one made out of straw . . .

I was just printing my final draft when Finn came home.

"Where have you been?" I asked.

"Nowhere," said Finn.

"Ah, I haven't been there in ages," I replied. "How is nowhere these days?"

Finn answered me with a glare.

"Hey, can I have the alarm clock?" I asked.

"I thought the glowing green numbers kept you awake and made you think of aliens."

"They do," I said. "But know what's worse than being kept awake by a somewhat illogical and completely embarrassing fear of space invaders? Worrying that I'm going to oversleep because you keep hitting the snooze button. Anyway, I have to get up extra early tomorrow."

"Fine." Finn headed over to his side of the room and unplugged the clock. "Here."

"Thanks," I said.

"Don't mention it," said Finn.

"Too late for that."

Finn noticed my book on Cindy Singer. "Oh, can I borrow that?" he asked.

"Sure," I said. "It's Mom's, and we're lucky she has it. The library had nothing."

"Mind if I check out your report, too?" he asked.

"Yes," I said, closing my laptop. "I do." I knew he'd peek as soon as I left our room, but I didn't care. I had bigger things to worry about.

Chapter 23

. . .

The next morning I woke up at six, showered, got dressed, and printed out a new copy of my report on Cindy Singer. (Turns out Finn had not only read my original copy, he'd also gotten chocolate fingerprints all over it.) Then I packed my backpack and headed out.

Prospect Park has off-leash hours every morning until nine. That meant any dog with any cred is out sniffing and running, fetching balls and sticks and Frisbees, picking fights, roaming in the grass, rolling in the dirt, and barking at everyone who walks by.

By seven o'clock I'd already spied bulldogs, pinschers, whippets, pugs, Labs, poodles, Shih Tzus, sheepdogs, rat terriers, beagles, hound dogs, and everything in between. The scene was complete and total Dogapalooza.

I explored the area near the Ninth Street entrance in search of Cindy Singer's house of straw. But all I found was a gigantic nest that had to belong to the monk para-keets. I could tell because it had lots of green feathers underneath.

I wondered if maybe I was wrong. Maybe Cindy considered this real house of straw—the one made by the actual birds that inspired her—to be a part of her exhibit. It kind of made sense. And it still jived with her numbers and fairy-tale themes. But why didn't she include it on the tour? I didn't know, and I was out of time. After taking a few pictures, I headed to school, disappointed that my big break was actually not so big. Or, for that matter, any kind of break.

When I was still a few blocks away, I noticed two people holding hands. They seemed to be about my age, which wasn't a big deal at all. But I couldn't help but stare, because from the back the guy looked kind of like my brother. He was tall and skinny, with Finn's same dark shaggy hair and the same backpack, too. Also, he walked like Finn, kind of slow and relaxed like he didn't have to be anywhere anytime soon.

And weirder than that, the girl looked a lot like Lulu, with long, dark, wavy hair pulled back in a Tuesday-violin-lesson single braid. She even had on Lulu's new brown boots. And she carried a violin case. And come to think of it, her walk seemed familiar, too.

But it couldn't be them, because, as I said, these

kids were holding hands, and that would mean . . . well, that would mean something I didn't want to think about.

Still, I couldn't help but speed up—just to rule out the possibility.

So I did. And that's when I realized it *was* Lulu and Finn, and they were, in fact, holding hands.

I could not believe it.

No, wait a second. I could totally believe it. Suddenly, so much made sense.

Lulu hanging out with my brother and giggling at everything he said.

Lulu asking Finn to be an extra on Seth Ryan's movie. And Finn saying yes!

Lulu not being around when I needed her.

Lulu being Lulu, instead of Lucy.

I ran to catch up to them, jumped into the street so I could pass by them, and then turned around. "Hey!" I said, surprising them both.

They dropped their hands, as if it wasn't too late. And we stared at one another, no one saying a word.

I was the first to break the silence when I shouted, "You guys are busted!"

Chapter 24

. . .

"I'm sorry you had to find out this way," Lulu whispered to me a few hours later. We sat next to each other in English. Obviously, because that's what best friends do—sit by each other and tell each other everything, including stuff about crushes and actual relationships and, wait a second . . .

"Please don't be mad," she continued. "You're my best friend, and I can't stand that you're mad at me."

I didn't want to pout in silence, but I couldn't figure out what to say. "I'm not mad," I insisted finally.

"Then why did you refuse to speak to us when you saw us on the street? Why did you run away?"

"Shock."

"So how come your nostrils were flaring?"

"Allergies?" I tried.

Lulu gave me a look that told me she didn't believe me.

"Look, I'm sorry, but I just don't understand why you didn't tell me about you and Finn. You're my best friend. He's my brother."

"And that's exactly why it's so complicated. Anyway, I did try to tell you."

"You did not!" I cried. "Okay, fine. Maybe I am mad. But only because I tell you everything. You were the first person to know I liked Milo, and I've asked you a gazillion times if you had a crush on anyone and you always said no."

"I've been wanting to tell you since this summer, but there was never a good time."

"You've liked my brother since the summer?"

"Yes," said Lulu.

"Have you guys been together that long?"

"No, it's still new. Our first kiss was just—"

"Aack!" I put my hands over my ears. "I don't want to hear it. Please don't ever talk about kissing my brother!"

"See," said Lulu, "that's exactly why I couldn't tell you anything before. It's too awkward."

I could see that she might have a point. I dropped my hands down to my sides and gave her a weak grin. "Okay, sorry about that. I'll try not to act so horrified, but please keep those kinds of details to yourself. And you keep saying you tried to tell me, but what I don't get is, why didn't you try harder? All you had to do was say it. We talk every day. Sometimes we talk six times a day."

Lulu huffed out a small breath as she rebraided her hair. "Every time Finn came up, you changed the subject. It's like you had this mental block. You didn't want to know."

"I don't know what you're talking about," I insisted.

Lulu looked at me. "Are you sure?"

I never got the chance to answer her, because class started. Not that I could focus or anything. Because the more I thought about it, the more I realized Lulu was right. This had been going on for a long time, and there were plenty of clues. I'd just chosen to ignore them.

Looking back, I now see that it all started with the scarf way back in September. Lulu knit one for Finn. But what she gave him was so much more than a scarf. What she did was tell him, *I don't want your neck to get cold this winter. And I care about your neck so much I'm going to spend hours knitting this for you. And I'm going to make it green and white striped—your favorite colors, even though they're Celtics colors and you're a fan of the Knicks. Yes, yarn is expensive, and I had to special-order the green and now I have all this extra and no other use for it, but that's okay. You're worth it.*

Lulu had been trying to tell me about Finn this whole time. Not with words, but with tiny gestures I should've picked up on.

It shook me, how I'd missed the obvious, even though

I'm supposed to be this super-observant detective. It made me wonder what else I was missing.

With Seth's disappearance and the dog-eggings, I mean. The house of straw had turned out to be a bust, but where else could I look? The egger had to be hiding somewhere. Was there a second straw house I hadn't noticed? And how come the egger stopped attacking dogs so suddenly after Seth disappeared? Was it merely because the neighborhood was crawling with cops and detectives? Or was there more to it?

And that's when this image popped into my brain: Jones Reynaldo. Or, more specifically, Jones Reynaldo's hair, and the random pieces of straw I noticed sticking out of it that first time I saw him.

Jenna Beasely had told me that Jones wanted a permit to shut down the park so he could keep the neighborhood dogs away from his shoot, and his permit had been rejected. But was Jones the type of guy to just give up? I didn't think so.

Knowing Jones, he probably tried to get rid of the dogs in some different way.

Which made me wonder: what if that straw in his hair wasn't so random after all?

Chapter 25

. . .

Whenever I tried to puzzle out the egger mystery, part of my brain kept telling me I should be focusing on Seth Ryan's disappearance. And when I tried to solve *that* mystery, another part of my brain reminded me of what Charlotte had said. There are a gazillion people looking for Seth Ryan, but no one but me looking out for the neighborhood dogs. Figuring out what to focus on seemed impossible. One thing I knew for sure, though, was that my clients needed to be walked. So that's what I did after school—as quickly as possible.

When I dropped off Preston that afternoon, Isabel was home and still packing.

"Did you find your other pink flamingo?" I asked.

"Oh, yes. It was in my storage space, right smack-dab in the middle of my collection of miniature tin soldiers. But I decided it would be a silly thing to bring to Paris," said Isabel as she tried—without much luck—to stuff a heavy-looking metal boxy thing into her pink leopard-print duffel bag. "There's only so much I can take, and I need to save space for the essentials."

"I see," I replied. "And, um, what is that you're packing now?"

"My espresso machine. I drink three cups a day, minimum, just to function. Didn't you know that? I thought everyone knew that about me."

"Aren't they famous for espresso in Paris?"

"That's cappuccino," said Isabel.

"Maybe you should drink that instead. You know—when in Rome."

"Rome is not in Paris, dear." Isabel stood and dusted her hands off on her zebra-striped bell-bottoms. "My goodness, what do they teach you in school these days? Not that I should talk. I went to a performing-arts school. My geography isn't so hot, either. But at least I learned to sing and dance."

To prove her point, she did a quick tap dance routine around her living room—shuffle, ball change, shuffle, ball change, finishing it off with some jazz hands and the tipping of an imaginary hat. "Ta-dah!" she shouted, and then waited for applause, except I wasn't in the mood. Her mention of geography had reminded me of Seth Ryan and made me feel bad that I hadn't yet tracked him down.

"I'm just using the expression 'when in Rome,'" I

clarified. "I realize you are not going to Rome, which is in Italy."

Isabel turned back to her suitcase. "Are you okay, dear? You seem a smidgen upset."

"I am, and more than a smidgen," I replied. "I thought I'd solved the dog-egger mystery this morning, but it turns out I was wrong. And if I can't track down one lousy egger, how am I supposed to find Seth Ryan?"

"Oh, you mean that young actor? I read about his disappearance in *The New York Times* this morning. Shame, it is. Poor boy. But why are you searching for him? The neighborhood is already crawling with private investigators. Is there some kind of reward involved?"

"No," I said. "It's just—well, I'm one of the last people to see him, and . . ."

"And you have a crush." Isabel clapped her hands together, delighted by the idea.

"No, that's not it," I replied emphatically. I didn't have a crush. Not on Seth Ryan, anyway . . .

"Maybe I can help," said Isabel.

I laughed, figuring she was joking, since Isabel needs help finding her glasses three times a day—except she seemed to be serious.

"I've read about your Seth Ryan. I haven't seen any of his films, but I know the type."

"And what type is that?" I asked, skeptical because

Seth wasn't a type. He was a boy, a beautiful, talented boy who could be in great danger this very moment. I doubted Isabel could help, and I didn't have time to waste. But I couldn't just say that. Not after Isabel plonked down on her overstuffed armchair with a small grunt.

"Let's see," she said. "He was discovered as a baby and grew up in the Hollywood system, and he's always been a star, correct?"

I nodded.

"Child actors have a strange existence. We expect them to act like regular kids on camera, but once the cameras stop rolling they must behave professionally, like adults. Turning it on and off like that can be confusing. Seth must have had an extremely unusual childhood. On the one hand, he got to see so much, but on the other hand, he had to sacrifice a lot, too—his regular freedoms, his normal childhood. These are things to keep in mind during your investigation."

I thought about Seth's T-shirt. How wearing it inside out and backward wasn't a fashion statement. He simply didn't know how to dress himself, because he usually had a stylist or a team of stylists or Fiona picking out his clothes.

Maybe Isabel did know what she was talking about. I pushed a pile of sweaters out of the way and sat down on her sofa. "That makes a lot of sense."

"How many films has this Seth Ryan been in?" she asked. "There's so much wonderful cinema out there; I have a hard time keeping track."

"I'm not sure. Probably about a dozen."

"Make a list and watch them," Isabel said, very matter-of-factly, like she was filling a prescription. As if watching Seth's movies would solve everything. As if watching Seth's movies would solve *anything*.

All my hope faded fast. "I'm sure it would be fun to have a Seth Ryan movie marathon, but I don't really have time for that right now. I fear that the longer he's gone, the less likely he is to be found, ever, and the more danger he could—never mind. I don't even want to go there. He's going to be found—he has to be. I'm just scared that if it doesn't happen soon, then—"

"Calm down, dear," said Isabel. "What I mean is, you should watch Seth's movies and search for clues within them. They're his whole life and everything he's ever known. Plus, life imitates art far more often than art imitates life. Do you know who said that?"

"Besides you?" I asked.

"Oscar Wilde," said Isabel. "The wonderful Irish writer and poet. Did I tell you about the time I was in *The Importance of Being Earnest*?"

"I think so," I said.

"It was in London, in 1974. A fine year. I had moved

there to star in a different West End play, one that never went up. I was sitting at a café, and who should walk by but—"

"Know what," I said, standing and heading for the door. "That makes sense. I think I'm going to take your suggestion and hit that video store now."

"Good," said Isabel. "And good luck."

"You, too," I replied. "And, seriously—leave the espresso machine at home. I'm sure they have fine coffee in Paris."

"You might be on to something," said Isabel. "I'm going to miss you, Maggie."

The video store had only three of Seth's movies: *Vampire's Retreat*, *Meet Me at Sunrise*, and an old one I'd never heard of called *Going Going Gone*. I rented them all. (Which also involved paying an extra ten bucks in late fees, thanks to Finn.)

Back at home I studied the list of credits. Brandon Wilson was in all three. In *Vampire's Retreat*, he played Seth's kid brother. In *Meet Me at Sunrise*, he played his best friend, and in *Going Going Gone*, his rival.

Since I'd just seen *Vampire's Retreat* last month, I turned on *Meet Me at Sunrise* and got comfortable. During one scene about halfway through the movie, I noticed Brandon in the background; he appeared to be sneering. Yet in the movie, he was supposed to be playing

Seth's loyal best friend. I'm surprised no one noticed and had him reshoot the scene. But more importantly, I wondered if Beatrix was right. Brandon probably *was* jealous of Seth's career. But did that give him motivation to make Seth disappear? And if so, what did he do with him? And how would I find him?

"What are you watching?" Finn asked when he came into the living room an hour later.

"*Meet Me at Sunrise*," I said. "But it just ended."

"So Milo's right. You *are* obsessed with Seth Ryan."

"Am not." I grabbed the remote and turned off the TV. "When did Milo say that?"

Finn shrugged. "I don't know. Yesterday, maybe?" He picked up the stack of DVDs and flipped through them. "So what's up with the Seth Ryan marathon? Are you missing Mister Lover Boy?"

"Do not sit there and make fun of me for having a crush on Seth Ryan, which I do not, while you've been going out with Lulu for who knows how long!"

"Okay, let's not talk about that," said Finn, turning red.

"Good idea," I replied. "And don't make fun of Seth. He's still missing, and I'm only trying to help."

"By sitting around watching a bunch of movies?"

"I'm looking for clues. And don't question my methods. How many dogs have you rescued?"

"Know how I always tell you you're being too modest?" asked Finn.

"Yup," I said.

"This is not one of those times."

"Have anything else helpful to add?" I asked.

"Nope." Finn flopped down on the couch and kicked off his shoes. "What's next? How about *Going Going Gone*? I've never heard of it."

"Me, neither. It's pretty old."

I turned on the movie, but only after making Finn promise to keep his mouth shut. Which he did—but maybe only because he fell asleep ten minutes into it. Which is too bad, because the movie was good. And weird.

And also? Strangely relevant.

Going Going Gone was about a child-genius computer programmer named Joe who was wanted by some international evildoers.

Early on in the story, he got kidnapped. His best friend, Riley, found a ransom note, and here's what it said: *We have the boy. Don't bother looking. You'll never find him.*

Yup, that's right. The ransom note in the movie matched Seth's ransom note in real life.

And suddenly, I had a feeling I knew exactly who wrote it.

Chapter 26

• • •

School seemed to last *forever* on Wednesday, like everyone was moving underwater, or in slow motion, or underwater *and* in slow motion. All I wanted to do was get through the day, walk my dogs, and figure out where Seth was hiding himself. Yup, that's right. Seth kidnapped himself. I was sure of it. It's the only thing that made sense, since the note was quoted verbatim.

Also, from different news accounts, I'd learned that when Seth was kidnapped, there was no sign of a struggle.

And thinking back to our conversation at the Pizza Den, he seemed like a guy who'd been wanting to disappear for a while. He'd practically said as much when he asked me if I ever wanted to walk away from my life.

That Seth Ryan had chosen to go into hiding was the only plausible theory. All I had to do was prove it. Oh, and find the guy.

The problem was, I didn't know where to look. After swearing my friends to secrecy, I told them about my theory, but no one had any great ideas. Lulu was too busy hanging out with Finn. Beatrix remained convinced Brandon was the bad guy, and Sonya began designing a line of Seth Ryan–inspired rescue wear practically before I finished explaining everything.

So I was on my own. When school ended, I raced around the neighborhood walking all of my dogs, saving Bean for last. When I took her outside, I found Milo sitting on the front stoop.

Boy-Milo.

Bean stopped to growl at his shoelaces and I remained silent, because what was there to say to the guy who'd been doing such an amazing job of ignoring me for so long?

"I like Bean's new sweater," Milo said after a minute of awkward silence. "Did Lucy make it?"

I shook my head and walked away because I couldn't just pretend like everything was still cool between us.

Milo scrambled to his feet and followed us. "She didn't?" he asked.

"No, not that. Yes—Lucy made the sweater, but we're not doing this. We can't pretend like everything is okay and that you haven't been acting totally weird all week."

"You think I've been acting weird? You're the one who's obsessed with Seth Ryan."

"I'm not obsessed. I'm just trying to find him because it's a mystery and that's what I do. You know that! But even if I were obsessed with Seth, what's wrong with that?"

Milo kicked a rock into the gutter. "You say that like we're not even together."

"We're not," I said, glancing at him.

Milo looked away, but not before I saw the disappointed look on his face.

"Are we?" I asked.

"I thought we were," he said finally.

"Oh." I paused. Not sure of what to say next, I kept walking.

Milo did, too—both of us moving fast, our strides in sync.

"We never really talked about it," I said. "So I didn't know."

"Well, what did you think? I just happened to be hanging around here after school every day? My chess tutor lives twelve blocks away."

"But your grandma had all those prescriptions."

"Her pharmacy delivers," Milo said. "Plus, it's nowhere near here."

"Well, why didn't you just tell me you were coming by to see me? Why did you always act like it was some crazy coincidence?"

"I thought you'd figure it out," said Milo. "It's like you said—you're the detective."

"You could've just told me you liked me."

"And you could've told me. But you didn't—and you never even called me when I asked you to."

This was true. But how could I tell him about my doubts? My whole fear of turning into Jasper Michaelson seemed even more ridiculous now. "You're right. I should've called. And you shouldn't have pretended you were accidentally always around."

"So how are the investigations?" he asked.

"Terrible. I've got no idea where Seth is, although I'm pretty sure I know what happened to him. And as for the egger, I think he's been hanging out in one of Cindy Singer's tree houses, but I can't find it."

"I thought those weren't open to the public," said Milo.

"The two we saw aren't, but I think she built a third one."

"Because she's always doing things in threes?" asked Milo.

"You knew about that, too?" I asked.

Milo nodded. "Ms. Murphy kind of hinted about it, and then when I was working on my report, it came up."

"I figured that out, too. And I got so excited when I thought I'd found the third house, the one made out of straw, except it was actually just the monk parakeets' nest."

Suddenly Milo stopped walking. "Where did you see a monk parakeet's nest?"

"In the park—over by the Ninth Street entrance."

"But that's impossible. The monk parakeets don't live in Prospect Park."

"Sure they do," I said.

"Have you ever seen one?" he asked.

"No," I replied carefully, trying to puzzle this all out. "But Cindy said so. I mean, I think she did, right? That's her whole inspiration." Even as I said the words, something seemed weird. "She did say they lived in Prospect Park, right?"

"Nope. She wouldn't have, because they don't," said Milo. "I know for a fact that the only monk parakeets in Brooklyn live in the Green-Wood Cemetery."

"Then who's using that nest by Ninth Street?" I asked.

And before I even finished the question, I realized I had my answer.

Chapter 27

. . .

"I've gotta go, okay? Here." I handed Milo Bean's leash, then thought better of it. Who knows what Cassie would do if I left her precious pup in the hands of someone else? Something told me she wouldn't be so understanding. "Never mind. I'll call you later—promise!" I took the leash back and raced Bean home.

Then I sprinted for the park. Back to the monk parakeets' nest, which obviously wasn't what it appeared to be, like so many things lately . . .

I entered at Ninth Street, and it didn't take long to find the "nest" again. Looking at it now, it certainly seemed big enough to hide in. And there wasn't a parrot in sight, only the same feathers from yesterday. Feathers Cindy probably put there so no one would find her tree house.

I circled the tree a few times, trying to figure out how

to get up. The lower branches were thick and spaced far apart. Climbing them wouldn't be easy, but I had no choice. If Jones Reynaldo could do it, I could, too.

Grabbing on to the lowest branch, I hoisted myself up. Or tried to, anyway. On my first two tries, I didn't make it. And once I did, I got stuck on my stomach, but only for a moment. "Oof!" I grunted, trying to maintain my balance as I swung one leg over the branch.

Once I was steady, I dusted my hands off on my jeans and looked around. A thick branch was just overhead, and I grabbed it with both hands and pulled again. Now that I was standing on the lowest branch, I found plenty more within reach. I climbed higher and higher until I finally made it to the structure. Close up, I could see it was merely a house made of wood and covered with a thick layer of straw. Luckily, there was a trap door at the bottom, which I opened pretty easily. Then, after some struggle, I managed to pull myself up inside.

"Hello?" I called, looking around at the messy, dark interior.

I spotted some empty bags of potato chips, discarded candy bar wrappers, three grease-stained pizza boxes, and a large stack of empty egg cartons. Also? One person huddled in the corner, trying to hide under his puffy red sleeping bag. Even though I'd climbed up in search of Jones Reynaldo, and had apparently found him, now that we were nearly face-to-face, I hesitated. Was confronting a temperamental, bratty director really the best idea? Especially considering the fact that I was alone and we were both about thirty feet in the air. Somehow I doubted it, but it was too late to turn back.

"Jones?" I asked, approaching carefully.

The figure shifted, but did not reveal himself right away.

"There's no point in trying to hide," I said, unable to keep my voice from wavering. "I know you're in there."

"Maggie Brooklyn?" he asked. His voice was muffled because of the sleeping bag, but he sounded *nothing* like Jones.

As I stepped closer, he lowered the sleeping bag. And I found myself looking right at Seth Ryan. He looked thin and pale. His shirt was covered in potato chips and his hair was messy. Not fashionably mussed; more like hadn't-been-brushed-in-days mussed.

I glanced from the empty egg cartons to Seth, my mind totally blown. "It was you?" I asked.

Chapter 28

* * *

"How did you find me?" asked Seth. "And what are you doing here?"

"Um, lucky accident," I replied, once I recovered from the shock. "I thought you were Jones."

"My director?" asked Seth.

"He's the only Jones I know."

"But why would you be looking for him up here?" asked Seth.

"Because he's the egger."

"The what?"

"Never mind," I said, shaking my head and trying to think straight. "I'll tell you later. Just as soon as you tell me something: why did you kidnap yourself?"

"All I wanted was to help the polar bears," Seth blurted out.

I blinked, figuring I must've misheard him. "You didn't just say 'polar bears,' did you?"

"Yes," said Seth. "You know how global warming is killing all these polar bears because their ice caps are melting and they're drowning?"

"I've read about that," I said, still puzzled.

"And have you seen pictures? It's terrible." Seth drew his knees up into his chest and hugged them, suddenly looking so young. He reminded me of a lost little kid hanging out in mall security, waiting to be rescued.

"You're telling me you wanted to go to Alaska to save these polar bears, and that's why you've been hiding in this tree house?" I asked, not quite following his logic.

"No, I wanted to run the LA Marathon for a charity that raises awareness of global warming," Seth explained. "But Fiona said I couldn't because of the security risk. I'm too high profile to participate in that kind of thing. She says all my running must be done in private on a treadmill in my own gym. Also, if people saw me sweat, it would be bad for my image."

"Huh," I replied, not knowing what else to say.

"I think it's the workout clothes she didn't approve of," Seth went on. "'Stars and spandex should never mix.' That's what she always said whenever she read about some other celebrity doing any sort of race."

"Workout clothes *are* pretty funny looking," I had to admit.

"Right." Seth nodded. "Anyway, Fiona told me to

donate money instead, which I did happily. And I'm glad I could help. It's just—I wanted to help in a different way, like a regular kid might. But Fiona says I'm a public person and I can't just do normal things. I have more responsibilities. People depend on me, and I must maintain my image."

This was all very interesting. And weird. But also, confusing. Seth's story simply didn't add up. Yes, he's a bizarre guy, but even this seemed too outlandish. Who runs away because of polar bears? There had to be more to the story.

"So global warming is what made you fake your own kidnapping and camp out in a secret tree house in the middle of a big movie shoot?" I asked, this being the first of my many, many questions.

"It's not just because of the polar bears. Other stuff has been getting to me, too." Seth shoved his sleeping bag aside, stood up, and stretched. "Things you wouldn't understand."

"Try me," I said.

"Well, for one thing, I just found out my dad has replaced me. And not just once."

"You mean because he had twins?" I asked.

"You knew?" The heartbreak in Seth's eyes was visible. "How did you know? I just found out about it— and not even from him. Jones asked me if my brothers were going to follow in my footsteps, because he needed babies for his next movie. I truly had no idea what he was talking about. It's crazy that my father didn't even tell me."

"Maybe he couldn't," I said. "You know, because of the restraining order."

"What restraining order?" asked Seth. He sat back down again and crossed his legs.

Did he honestly not know? "The one you filed against your father," I said gently.

Seth seemed shocked. "I never did that!"

"Someone did, and they signed your name. It's a matter of public record. That's what I read, anyway. Maybe Fiona is responsible? I'm guessing she thought it was necessary because your dad was stealing from you."

"But my dad never stole from me!" Seth cried.

"Then what was the custody battle all about?" I wondered.

Seth shook his head, a pained expression on his face. "I don't even know anymore; everything got so complicated. We got in a stupid fight. I wanted to do this movie in Japan and my dad wanted me to take a break, to move with him back home to Buffalo."

"He wanted you to quit acting?" I asked.

"Sort of. For a while, anyway. He thought I should finish sixth grade at a regular school because my tutors weren't teaching me enough."

"And you didn't want to go?"

"No way. I love acting. It's this incredible adventure, and I just feel like I'm doing what I was born to do."

"That's cool," I said, noticing Seth's eyes light up for the very first time.

"And it's fun, for the most part. Also, I know I need to be grateful. There are plenty of talented people out there who haven't gotten the breaks I have. I'm lucky it's worked out, but still, sometimes it all just gets to me. Not being able to walk down the street like everyone else, not getting to run in marathons or save the polar bears. Fiona thinks I'm ridiculous, but my dad understood. He feared I was missing out on too much. He always talked about how disappointed he was when I had to quit Little League to go film my first movie in LA. I never told him I was actually relieved because I can't stand baseball. I'd rather act than compete in sports. And I could never move back to Buffalo and go to a normal junior high school. I'd get beat up, stuffed into lockers. Guys would steal my lunch money."

Seth spoke so fast and so randomly I could barely follow him.

"Wait, why do you think people would steal your lunch money?"

"Because it happens all the time," Seth practically shouted.

"Where?" I asked.

"In school. I know what really happens because I starred in *Sixth Grade Confidential*, and I can't handle it." Seth was emphatic.

The movie he referred to was basically a *Diary of a Wimpy Kid* rip-off, about a nerdy kid who always got picked on. Except it wasn't a reality show or anything—it was a total comedy, very loosely based on middle-school life and exaggerated by at least a hundred times for laughs. In other words, it was a silly movie—at least to everyone else in the world.

It's funny how Isabel had predicted this. Seth really had grown up in the movies, and he had no idea what regular life was like. How there's not this total divide between nerds and jocks, how real life isn't all about being popular and sitting at the cool table, but about having friends who are true—friends you can be yourself with.

Poor Seth probably had no real friends—just a manager who lied to him and a director who bossed him around, a father who let him slip away . . .

But how could I explain all that? "*Sixth Grade Confidential* was just a silly comedy. School isn't really like that."

"That's what my dad told me, but why should I listen to him? After I chose acting over Buffalo, he disappeared."

"He was required by law to stay away from you," I reminded him. "The restraining order?"

"But no one told me, and I swear I never signed the thing. At least not knowingly."

"Do you think maybe Fiona tricked you into it?" I wondered.

"It's possible," Seth said with a sigh. "She has me sign things all the time. I don't always read them, so I guess it's my fault."

"I think this was all a big misunderstanding. I think your father does care about you. At least I assume that's why he wrote you this." I handed Seth the letter. "I found it in Fiona's purse. It's addressed to you, and I'm guessing you never received it."

Seth turned the envelope over in his hands. "I haven't heard from my father in over a year. He never even told me he got remarried."

"I'm so sorry," I said.

Seth ripped open the letter and read through it quickly. He looked up at me for a second and opened his mouth as if about to say something, but changed his mind. When he read the letter again, I saw tears well up in his eyes.

Finally he spoke. "He says he's been writing to me once a week for over a year. Ever since the courts ruled in Fiona's favor. And he's been numbering them." Seth pointed to the small number at the top of the page. "This is sixty-seven. He said he's going to keep writing until I respond. Even if it takes forever. Even if it's never."

"There's a sixty-seven on the envelope, too," I said. "I wondered what it meant. And are you telling me you didn't get any of the other sixty-six letters?"

Seth shook his head slowly, the horrible reality dawning on him. "I guess Fiona's been keeping them all from me." He rubbed his eyes and took a deep, shaking breath. And then the tears began to fall.

Seeing him so distraught made me cry, too. I couldn't help myself. This was all too terrible. I couldn't believe that just yesterday I'd felt sorry for Fiona, when she didn't truly care about Seth. No one who cared about him would keep him from his own father. Yet she'd been making that choice every single day—for sixty-seven weeks so far.

"How about we get out of this tree and find a phone and give him a call?" I asked.

Seth smiled at me, wiped his tears with the back of his hand, and sniffed. "That's a great idea."

Once we were on solid ground, I asked, "How did you end up here, anyway?"

"I'm not allowed to say."

I watched Seth carefully and asked, "Does it have anything to do with Jones Reynaldo?"

He didn't try to deny it.

"Please don't tell anyone. I don't want him getting in trouble. It was cool of him to let me hide out here. He was only trying to help. He didn't need me for a few days and saw that I was stressed and could use some time to chill. He also said it would be a fun prank and good publicity for his movie, too. A total win-win."

"A fun prank?" I knew Jones was a bad guy, but this was a new level of awful. "Do you know how many people have been looking for you? There's an international search! And guess what Jones was using this space for before you got here."

Seth looked up at the tree house, confused. "I know he's friends with the artist who built this place. But I didn't know he spent any time up here."

"Didn't you notice all those empty egg cartons?" I asked. "He's been egging local dogs—trying to scare them out of the park so he could film here."

Seth's entire face darkened. "What?" he asked.

"Let's go," I said. "I'll tell you all about it on the way."

Chapter 29

• • •

I took Seth home and introduced him to my parents. They wanted to call the police immediately, but I convinced them to wait a little while until he had the chance to at least call his dad.

Seth took the phone into my room for privacy and came back five minutes later with the biggest smile on his face. "My dad's getting on a plane right now and flying down here," he told me. "And after I finish this movie, I'm going home to Buffalo to meet my brothers. I might even stay for a while. My dad says whatever I want—it's up to me."

"That's fantastic," I said, giving Seth a hug. "Are you ready to go to Second Street?"

"Oh, I don't need to be at work until tomorrow morning."

"But you need to talk to Fiona," I said. "Tell her you're not going to let her push you around anymore."

Seth shook his head. "No need. My dad's taking care of the Fiona mess. He's probably on the phone with the police this very second."

"Well, what about Jones, then?"

"What about him?" asked Seth.

"Don't you want to tell him off?" I asked.

Seth giggled nervously. "Why would I do that? He's my director."

Uh-oh. It's like he was brainwashed or something. How could I make him snap out of it? "You can't let him get away with this. Think about the dogs. Or don't— think about yourself and about all the people who've lied to you and misled you. You've got to stand up for yourself. This is your big chance."

Seth couldn't argue with me, because I wouldn't let him. This was too important. He was going to Second Street and he was going to stand up for himself, even if I had to drag him there. And it turns out I practically did.

Five minutes later, we stood on the corner watching Jones yell at poor Zander, the props guy.

Seth put his hand on my shoulder and whispered in my ear. "He seems pretty mad. Maybe we should come back later. Don't you think?"

"There is no later," I told him. "Only now."

Seth took a deep breath and clenched his fists. "I'm going in," he said, and walked right up to Jones and tapped him on the shoulder.

"Hold on a second," Jones snapped without even turning around.

"I don't have a second," said Seth.

When Jones turned around, his face betrayed his true emotions. I saw shock and fear, but only for a moment. Then his expression turned joyful. "You're back. You've escaped! I've been so worried. What happened to you?"

"I faked my own kidnapping and you helped me, remember? You even showed me where to hide, and you've been having Zander bring me food twice a day."

"Um, can we talk in private?" Jones asked, trying to lead Seth away from the very interested crowd that had gathered.

"Sure," said Seth, staying put and raising his voice so everyone around could hear. "After you tell me why you've been egging the neighborhood dogs."

Someone gasped. Seth glanced toward the small crowd. Realizing he had an audience seemed to fuel his fire. I saw a glint in his eye, a slight smile tugging at the corners of his mouth before he turned ruthless.

"Or should I just go to the police?" asked Seth. "I'm happy to do that right now."

"No, no, no," Jones said, smiling at Seth. "Please don't do that. I can explain. I just need a—"

"Save it!" said Seth, holding up his hand. "There is no explanation. What you did was insane and insanely horrible, and you're going to make it right. And here's how. First, you're going to track down each of the dogs you egged and apologize to them and to their owners. Then you're going to make large donations to every single animal shelter in Brooklyn."

"How large?" asked Jones.

Seth smiled. "You're going to donate your entire salary for this movie."

Jones's eyes widened. "But that's . . . you can't . . . there's no way you can—"

"I can and I just did and guess what? I'm not even done here."

Someone from the crowd let out a whoop.

Seth ignored the guy and continued speaking. "You're also going to wrap up this shoot and move out of Brooklyn immediately."

"But we're not finished," said Jones.

"You are," said Seth. "You've been finished since the moment you let that first egg fly. You do not deserve to be in Brooklyn, and you've got to stay away from Brooklyn's dogs. Understand?"

Jones nodded, finally scared silent, listening because he had no choice.

As I stood on the sidelines and watched this all go down, something occurred to me. Like the monk parakeets who escaped captivity and found their freedom in

Brooklyn, Seth gained his freedom here, too. By hiding in their fake nest, he was able to avoid his own celebrity. And once he was pushed out of that nest (sort of), he finally learned how to fly.

(I'm talking figuratively here.)

Anyway, once Seth finally finished chewing out Jones, the entire crowd cheered. And while this seems like the perfect Hollywood ending, it's actually even better, because this story isn't over.

Chapter 30

• • •

"So you caught the egger," Charlotte said to me at school the next day. "Very cool. And I'm glad your boyfriend turned up, too."

"So am I," I replied. "His name is Milo Sanchez. You've probably seen him around here. Tall, cute, brown floppy hair, great at chess."

Charlotte tilted her head and stared. "You and Seth broke up?" she asked.

I smiled. "It's a little more complicated than that. Let's just say we agreed to stay friends."

"That's cool." Charlotte shrugged. "Anyway, I just wanted to say thanks for finding Mister Fru Fru's egger."

"It's what I do," I replied.

"Yeah, I know, and I'm impressed." Charlotte turned around and left without another word.

And life went on as usual. I walked my dogs. I solved mysteries. I even got used to Finn and Lulu.

And six months later, I went to Hollywood.

No, not to live. That would be insane! How could I leave Brooklyn when it's my middle name? I can't. It'll never happen. I mean I headed to Hollywood for a week—for Seth Ryan's film premiere. Yup, that's right—*Vanished* was finally done.

Seth had moved up to Montreal for a while to finish filming. We'd been pen pals ever since he left town.

That's how I knew that after he finished working on the movie, he'd decided to take some time off and hang out in Buffalo with his family. Seth refused to enroll in regular school, but he agreed to resume his studies with a real tutor—one that would at least teach him the difference between a borough and a city. (I hoped.)

And last month, Seth surprised me by sending first-class tickets to Hollywood for my whole family—tickets that I promptly traded in for coach seats so I'd have enough money to fly my friends out, too.

Yes, flying first class would've been cool, but not as cool as bringing my best friends along with me.

In fact, all six of us were in the same row. Me, Milo, Lulu, Finn, Beatrix, and Sonya.

(My parents were nice enough to sit a few rows up, out of sight.)

It felt funny but at the same time totally perfect to have everyone here with me. Beatrix and Sonya wore their new "Brooklyn Barks for Seth Ryan" T-shirts. Finn consoled Lulu, who was upset because they'd confiscated her favorite knitting needles back at security. And once the pilot announced we were ready for takeoff, Milo got way fidgety.

"You okay?" I asked.

"Fine!" he said, a little too fast.

"It's gonna be fun!" I said. "Don't worry."

He'd only agreed to come on the condition that I would sit next to him on the plane. He'd never been on a real one before, and he was scared of flying.

That's why I reached for his hand and held it, to calm him down.

He seemed okay, and before I knew it, we were soaring through the air. Once we'd reached cruising altitude, the pilot turned off the seat-belt sign with a ding.

Milo turned to me. "Guess what?" he said.

"What?" I asked.

"I'm just kidding. This isn't my first airplane trip, and I'm not scared of flying. I actually kind of love it."

I narrowed my eyes at him, trying to figure him out, but Milo is not an easy boy to figure out. That's why I decided to just ask him, straight out. "Then why did you tell me you were scared?"

He grinned. "Because I wanted an excuse to hold your hand."

I looked down at our interlaced fingers and gave his hand a little squeeze. "Guess what?" I said, leaning my head on his shoulder. "You didn't need an excuse."

Acknowledgments

• • •

Thanks very much to everyone at Bloomsbury. You are all amazing! I'm also very grateful to Laura Langlie and Bill Contardi.

I could not have done this without the love and support of my family, Leo, Lucy, and Jim. I'm also so grateful to my friends, advisors, and early readers, including Coe Booth, Sarah Mlynowski, Jessica Ziegler, and Ethan Wolff.

It seems strange to mention my neighborhood and dog, but without Brooklyn or Aunt Blanche, this series would not exist. So thank you for the inspiration!

Annabelle faces her toughest challenge yet:
choosing which of her friends
is the most talented!

From the author of *Boys Are Dogs*

ONE TOUGH CHICK

Leslie Margolis

BLOOMSBURY

When Annabelle's school puts on a talent show, she's
named one of the judges. Which is perfect . . .
until her friends accuse her of playing favorites. Can she
remain a fair judge without hurting anyone's feelings? It'll
take one tough chick to get through this tricky situation.

Read on for a sneak peek!

I hopped on my bike.

"Say hi to Oliver for us," said Emma.

Simply hearing Emma say Oliver's name made me feel all nervous and jumpy. Which is exactly how I felt about Oliver himself.

He's in the sixth grade, too. We sit next to each other in science, and we've been friends for a while. Here's what I know about him so far: He's short and sweet and cute. He's a good student, with excellent penmanship, and he loves to draw. Actually, Oliver loves all sorts of art. He takes private painting classes, and he and his parents go to museums for fun. Oliver's mom is from Jamaica and his dad is from England. He's black and he's got a slight Jamaican accent. Oliver, I mean. His dad is white. His mom is black. And they both have accents, too. Oliver plays cricket and calls dinnertime "tea" and goes to the West Indian Day parade downtown every single year and packs Jamaican patties in his lunch sometimes.

I don't remember the exact moment I fell for him.

My crush didn't come instantaneously, like how sometimes you're stuck on one question on a test and then suddenly the answer pops into your brain—seemingly out of thin air.

I've probably always liked him on some level, but it was more of a below-the-surface type of thing, always lurking, like dust bunnies under my bed. Not to compare Oliver to dust bunnies. He's much cuter and he's never made me sneeze.

Anyway, I don't know how long Oliver has liked me. Or if he even does like me as more than a friend and a lab partner.

All I know is tonight is the night we are going out on our first official date.

I think.

I mean I know we're going out. I'm just not 100 percent positive it's what I should call a date.

Here is what I do know:

1. Oliver and I are going out for pancakes.
2. We are going out for pancakes because Oliver invited me out for pancakes.
3. Oliver invited me in order to celebrate our team's second-place win in Birchwood Middle School's Sixth-Grade Science Fair.
4. The second-place prize was gift certificates to the International House of Pancakes.
5. Oliver did not invite our third lab partner, Tobias, because he's allergic to pancakes.

That's what Oliver told me, anyway. Which leads me to my final and most important point in regard to this matter.

6. Tobias is NOT allergic to pancakes.

I know this because I conducted an experiment last week. I sat down next to Tobias at lunch and asked if it was okay to eat a sandwich next to him.

"What do you mean?" asked Tobias, glaring at me suspiciously. "Are you going to chew with your mouth open or drool or spit your food out like some old geezer with no teeth?"

Tobias is kind of obnoxious in case you can't tell based on the above interaction.

"Nope," I said. "And I think what you just said is offensive to old geezers. My grandma is old and her table manners are impeccable. Plus, you'd never even know she wore dentures."

Tobias scowled (he's very good at scowling) and brushed his dark brown bangs off his greasy, somewhat pimply forehead. "What's your point, Spazabelle?"

"Didn't we decide you weren't allowed to call me that anymore?" I asked, flicking his ear with my finger.

"Ow!" said Tobias.

"You totally deserved that," I replied. "I have no remorse."

"Fine," he grumbled, all sulky, frowning down at his lunch. "Now why are you here again?"

"I want to make sure I can sit here and eat bread next to you, that you're not allergic to wheat."

"And why would I be allergic to wheat?" Tobias asked.

"I don't know. I'm just checking. Celiac disease—that's what it's called when you can't eat wheat—is very big now."

"Well, I don't have it."

"Good," I said. "Are you allergic to anything else?"

"Dust," said Tobias, rubbing his nose subconsciously. "It makes me sneeze."

"Duh—everyone is allergic to dust," I said. "I mean do you have any food allergies? Wheat, peanut butter, nuts, strawberries, pancakes—"

"Pancakes?" asked Tobias. "Are you joking?"

I shook my head no. "So you're telling me you are not and have never been allergic to pancakes, correct?"

"Are you trying to get me to fork over my gift certificate?" he asked. "Because it ain't happening. I already went to the IHOP with my dad last week and it was awesome."

It took a lot to refrain from jumping up for joy. "So you already ate your pancakes?" I asked, needing confirmation.

"Did you take a stupid pill this morning?" asked Tobias. "Because you really seem to be missing something."

I was so excited I almost kissed him. Except not really. That would be gross. And I should be careful about what I say because kissing has been on my mind a lot lately. Except not in reference to Tobias, of course.

The thing is out of my four best friends—Rachel, Emma, Claire, and Yumi—I'm the only one of us who hasn't ever kissed a boy. And I want to—not just because my friends have kissed boys and I'm a follower. I'm not. And it's not merely because I feel a little left out, although I sometimes do feel that way, especially when they talk about kissing, which isn't that often, only sometimes, but enough. It's just I finally found a boy I want to kiss: Oliver. And I hope he wants to kiss me, too.

Anyway, instead of kissing Tobias (blech!), I gave him a goofy grin and said, "Thanks, dude."

As I was leaving Tobias called after me. "I thought you wanted to eat your sandwich here."

"I changed my mind," I said with a wave. "See you in science."

"Whatever." Tobias turned back to his food and grumbled something about girls being weird.

Just then I thought of another point: Even if Tobias were allergic to pancakes (and maybe embarrassed to admit it to me), I am sure he would be able to find something else to eat. The IHOP sells fruit and lots of breakfast meats: sausage and bacon and even turkey bacon.

As soon as I got home I parked my bike in the garage, took off my helmet, and bounced inside, up to my room.

I turned on The Beach Boys' *Pet Sounds*. My uncle

gave it to me for Christmas. He's always giving me music: Prince, the Beatles, the Rolling Stones, Velvet Underground, the Pixies, Patti Smith, and early Madonna. Most of it's good. And it's important to him that my iPod is eclectic and contains more than the usual Top 40 stuff and random '80s hits my friends listen to. Not that there's anything wrong with that stuff, either. I love it all.

Anyway, I skipped ahead to my favorite song on the CD—"Hang on to Your Ego." The entire song seemed perfect for this situation. It made me feel so very "I'm getting ready for a big night just like a real teenager from some movie would."

Then I turned to my closet, but before I even opened it my friend Claire called.

"Great timing," I said as soon as I picked up the phone. "Oliver will be here in less than an hour and I've got no idea what to wear."

Claire is a total fashion maven, so she's the perfect person to help me with this matter. But the silence on the other end of the line reminded me that Claire also likes Oliver. At least she used to like him. Claire and Oliver even went to the Valentine's Day dance together last month. And it was at the dance that Claire realized Oliver liked her just as a friend.

"I'm sorry, Claire. Was that super-insensitive and cruel of me to ask you for help getting ready for my date with Oliver?"

"No no no!" said Claire. "I'm just trying to picture your closet."

"Are you sure you're okay with this?" I asked.

"Totally," said Claire. "I'm calling to wish you luck tonight. It's going to be awesome and there are no hard feelings. I promise. If I can't go out with Oliver, I want you to."

"You're the best," I said.

"I know," said Claire. "Now tell me what you're thinking of."

I walked over to my closet and opened up the double doors. "I definitely don't want to wear jeans and a T-shirt because he sees me in that every day at school. But I don't want to get dressed up, either, because then I'd look like I'm trying too hard."

"Why don't you wear your black miniskirt with your charcoal leggings? The leggings say, 'This is not a date,' and the skirt says, 'It's the weekend and I want to look good for myself, not necessarily for anyone else.'"

"Wow, I didn't realize my clothes could say so much," I said.

"Don't make fun—this is important!" said Claire.

"Okay," I said. "Hold on." I put the phone down and tried on the skirt and leggings. Not bad. Then I put on a gray-and-black-striped shirt to go with it. After I got back on the phone I said, "You're right. This is perfect. I'm ready. Thanks."

"Wait!" Claire yelled. "What are you wearing on top?"

"My gray-and-black-striped T-shirt," I said. "It goes perfectly. You'd be proud."

"No, that's no good. With all that black and gray you must look like the grim reaper. And who wants to date the grim reaper?"

"Mr. Grim Reaper?" I said.

"Exactly—and that is not Oliver. Try something brighter. How about red?"

"Really?" I asked.

"Yeah, what's wrong with red?"

"Hearts are red. Lips, too."

"Yeah, and this is your first date, so red makes perfect sense. Come on—it'll be hot and you definitely want to be on fire."

"I do?" I asked. "I'm not even sure what that means, but hold on."

I searched through the laundry basket at the bottom of my closet. The clothes were all clean. My mom does my laundry but it's my job to put my stuff away. And usually I don't bother. Luckily I found the shirt at the bottom of the pile. And Claire was right. It looked good.

"Much better," I told her when I got back on the phone. "But are you sure it's not too dressy?"

"Not at all," said Claire. "If you were going over to Rachel's to watch *Mean Girls* for the hundred and thirteenth time, you still might wear a skirt if it happened to be a Saturday night because that's the kind of girl you are."

"Good to know. Thanks," I said. "I'd better go."

"Shoes!" Claire said. "Try on those knee-length

patent-leather boots I made you get at the mall last weekend. They'll be perfect! And have fun!"

"Thanks!" I hung up, put on my shoes, turned off the Beach Boys, and put on KT Tunstall's "Suddenly I See." Then I turned up the volume and bounced around my room as I brushed my hair.

Next I took out my makeup case, unzipped it, and lined up everything on my dresser. Then I realized I really needed better light for makeup application, so I put everything back in its case and carried it into the bathroom, where I unpacked it again, feeling a little silly for this rookie mistake. The entire world of makeup is new to me. Also, I'm more of an occasional traveler and I don't think I'll ever be a full-time resident.

Anyway, I have three different colors of lip gloss—pink, hot pink, and frosty pink with sparkles. My eye shadow case has twelve different shades of green, blue, violet, and gray. I also have blush, although my cheeks are fairly rosy, anyway, so I don't actually need it. It came with the eye shadow, though. Oh, and nail polish, except I never wear it because I think it looks weird and smells icky.

I brushed on some light-blue eye shadow and then applied the regular pink lip gloss, and just because I thought it would help, I used some blush. Staring at myself in the mirror I realized three things.

One: I did not look like myself.

Two: I looked like a sunburned alien with fish lips.

And three: That is certainly not the look I wanted to be sporting tonight.

I wiped off all the makeup with a damp wash-cloth and looked at myself again. Now I looked human, although a little red from the face scrub.

I stared at myself in the mirror from different angles. I put my hair up and let it fall down around my shoulders again. Then I practiced smiling.

Big smile.

Little smile.

Littler smile.

Tiny smile.

Teensy-tiny smile.

Toothy smile.

Super-toothy smile that actually made me look like a scary clown.

Closemouthed Mona Lisa smile. Weirdness!

And best of all, a regular casual smile.

I think I looked good.

My hair is long and straight and blond. I have dark-brown eyes and teeth that are almost straight but not quite.

I'm skinny but not scrawny except for my knees, which are a little knobby. I'm also shorter than your average sixth grader. Then again, so is Oliver. He's taller than me but just barely.

Looking at myself in the mirror again, I decided to reapply the lip gloss. Now my shiny pale pink lips looked nice, but were they too shiny? Did I want to draw attention to that part of my body?

Perhaps I did.

Kissing Oliver seemed like it would be fun and exciting. Kissing seemed kind of scary, too.

I locked the bathroom door and looked at myself some more. This time I puckered up my lips. They looked weird and guppylike.

I wondered if Oliver would be my first kiss. I wondered if it would happen tonight. Did I even want it to happen tonight? Is it okay to kiss on the first date? Is it okay to kiss if you don't even know if you're actually *having* a date?

I checked my watch. It was still five o'clock. How was it still five o'clock when I got home from the park at five?

Wait—the second hand on my watch looked frozen. I shook my watch and stared some more. Nothing moved. There were two possibilities.

1. Time had stopped while I'd kept moving.
2. My watch was broken.

"Honey, what time did you say Oliver was picking you up?" my mom asked.

"Six thirty," I said. "Why? What time is it?"

"Six thirty," she said.

"What?" I asked. "You're kidding. Don't say that."

"Please don't yell at me."

"I'm not yelling," I yelled. Then I added, "Sorry." I ran out of the bathroom and back into my room, flung open my closet and tore through it again, making sure I hadn't overlooked the perfect outfit.

"You look great, Annabelle. Don't worry."

"Who said I'm worried?" I screamed. "Do I look worried?"

My mom raised her eyebrows at me, something I found irritating to a crazy degree.

"Don't ask any more questions," I yelled before she even had a chance to speak. Yes, I realized that she hadn't actually asked me anything. She'd just offered some commentary, but I didn't want to correct myself. And I blamed her for this mistake, too. My mom who stood there smiling at me with her mouth closed, doing exactly what I'd asked her to do—nothing. Yet somehow even this annoyed me.

"And what are you wearing?" I asked.

"Yoga clothes," she replied.

For some reason I didn't want Oliver seeing my mom in yoga pants. They were just so . . . tight. And how come her hair looked so messy? Had she even brushed it today?

"When was the last time you got a haircut?" I asked.

"Annabelle, please calm down. Everything is going to be fine."

"But aren't you going to change before Oliver comes?" I asked, panicked.

"Why? I'm not going out with him. Or do you want me to come along, too?" she said, and laughed. "I haven't been to the IHOP in ages."

"Not funny!" I said. Then something else occurred to me. "*Why* are you wearing yoga clothes?"

"Well, most people who wear yoga clothes do so because they're about to take a yoga class. And it turns out I'm no exception." She said it like that was the most natural thing in the world for her to go to yoga on a Saturday night, but I knew better. My mom and yoga were like oil and water. Fire and ice. Peanut butter . . . and whatever doesn't go well with peanut butter.

What doesn't go with peanut butter?

Everything tastes better with peanut butter. I quickly ran through some food options: chocolate, bread, celery, apples . . .

Cheese! Cheese and peanut butter do not go well together. My mom and yoga were like cheese and peanut butter—a disastrous combination.

"You always said you hated yoga," I said. "Something about all those people sweating and grunting in one room seemed . . . did you call it 'unsavory'?"

"I may have but I recently realized that I've never even tried yoga."

"Did Ted talk you into this?" I asked.

My stepdad is a total fitness nut. He's been training for the LA marathon for months and the race is only two weeks away.

"Ted has nothing to do with it," my mom insisted. "Anyway, I just came in to wish you luck."

"Luck? You think I need luck?" For some reason my voice came out in a squeaky shout.

"No, Annabelle. I shouldn't have said that. You'll be fine with or without luck. Just relax and be yourself."

My self was a nervous wreck. My hands were sweaty and my pulse raced.

Mom kissed me on the forehead before she left. "I'll see you later. Remember—your curfew is nine o'clock, and if you leave the mall you'll have to call me."

"We're not even going to the mall!" I reminded her. "We're going to the IHOP. You know that! You just made a bad joke about joining us there."

"Was the joke really that bad?" She blinked at me, a little insulted.

I threw up my hands in an exaggerated shrug. "Do I really need to answer that?"

"Oh, never mind. I don't know where my brain has been these days." My mom left me alone—finally.

I turned back to the mirror. I could hardly believe that this might very well be my first real date with my soon-to-be first boyfriend.

It made me feel mature.

Sophisticated.

Oh, and scared out of my wits.

Which is a weird expression. What is a wit, exactly?

I changed watches. Luckily my other one—a Mickey Mouse watch my grandma got me at Disneyland—worked great.

Now that I knew it was six thirty-three and Oliver would be arriving at any moment, I didn't know what to do with myself.

Then I noticed my new camera sitting on my

bedside table. Ted had given it to me because he'd gotten a newer model. I picked it up and snapped a picture of myself in the mirror, figuring if this does turn out to be my first real date, if Oliver does turn out to be my first real boyfriend, I should document it.

When the doorbell chimed, my stomach jumped. I put my camera on my desk.

My hands shook. I clenched my fists so they'd stop but it didn't work.

I sneaked down the hall, all the way to the head of the staircase with my back flat against the wall, like a spy. Then I peeked around the corner. Oliver stood in the entryway with Ted, who shook his hand.

Spying on my stepdad from the top of the steps made me cringe. Ted's voice seemed too loud, his head especially bald and shiny.

I thought maybe I should remind Oliver that we weren't related by blood and he didn't even raise me or anything. I had only met Ted a year and a half ago.

Then I felt guilty because as dorky as he is, Ted's a sweet guy. It's not his fault he's dorky. Some people are born that way, I think.

It just happens, the way some people are blond and some people are brunette. Except that's not a very good comparison because, as we learned in science, hair color has to do with genetics and dorkiness probably does not. Plus Ted is bald.

I took a deep breath, resisted the temptation to look in the mirror again, and walked downstairs, silently reminding myself not to trip.

I smiled while at the same time worrying that my smile seemed too big and goofy. But it turns out I didn't have to worry because Oliver cracked a goofy smile right back at me.

Also? He wore khakis and a purple shirt with a collar. My point is not that he looked super-cute, although he did. It's this: Oliver got dressed up, too.

And his hair seemed shorter. Had he gotten a haircut for our date?

Did a shirt with a collar and khaki pants and a haircut make this a date? Or simply a Saturday night dinner between friends?

"Ready?" I asked.

"Sure thing," said Oliver. "Let's go."

"Have fun," my mom said. She must've sneaked in from the kitchen—I didn't even see her coming. And thankfully she'd thrown on jeans and a button-down shirt.

"Bye," I said.

As Oliver and I headed out the door all I could think was this: *It's go time!*

Photo: Jimmy Bruch

Leslie Margolis is the author of many books for young readers, including the first Maggie Brooklyn Mystery, *Girl's Best Friend*, as well as four books in the Annabelle Unleashed series. She lives with her family in Los Angeles, California. Please visit her online at www.lesliemargolis.com or www.maggiebrooklyn.com.

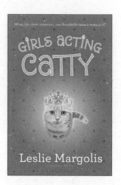